TRANSCENDENCE

DANIELLE ACKLEY-McPHAIL

Pennsville, NJ

PUBLISHED BY
Paper Phoenix Press
A division of eSpec Books
PO Box 242
Pennsville, NJ 08070
www.paperphoenixpress.com
www.especbooks.com

ISBN: 978-1-942990-63-5
ISBN (ebook): 978-1-942990-64-2

Previously published in an earlier version by Dark Quest Books, 2015.

Cover Art: woman eyes on cosmic background © Jozef Klopacka, www.shutterstock.com
Interior Art: Angel © Misha, www.fotolia.com

Copyeditor: Greg Schauer
Interior Design: Danielle McPhail
Sidhe na Daire Multimedia
www.sidhenadaire.com

ACKNOWLEDGEMENTS

My thanks go to Jennifer Brozek, John G. Hartness, John Grant, L. Jagi Lamplighter, Misty Massey, Lillian Cohen-Moore, the late CJ Henderson, Tonia Brown, Gail Z. Martin, and Paul Levinson for the wonderful introductions they have provided for this collection. I am honored by their words.

PREVIOUS PUBLICATIONS

Skippy and *Ruby Red* each first appeared in *Trails of Indiscretion* Magazine, published by Fortress Publishing.

Dervish first appeared in *Nth Degree* Magazine.

The Kindly One first appeared in *Dark Furies*, published by Die! Monster, Die! Books.

If I Had the Chance first appeared in the BSFAN Magazine, published by the Baltimore Science Fiction Society.

Beloved first appeared in *Bad-Ass Faeries*, published by Marietta Publishing; republished by Mundania Press.

The Misses Moirai first appeared in *Speculations from New Jersey*, published by The Garden State Speculative Fiction Writers.

Luna and *Portrait of a Green Mother* each first appeared in *Children of Morpheus*, published by Lite Circle Books.

Purgatory first appeared in *Hear Them Roar*, published by Spyre Publishing, republished by Marietta Publishing.

Stoli and Solitude first appeared in Tales of the Talisman Magazine.

Emberling first appeared in *Dragon's Lure*, published by Dark Quest Books.

Transcendence (under the title *A Legacy of Stars*) first appeared in *A Legacy of Stars*, published by Dark Quest Books.

IV   TRANSCENDENCE

On the Wings of An Angel first appeared in *In an Iron Cage: The Magic of Steampunk*, published by Dark Quest Books.

CONTENTS

DEDICATION

To my bygone friend, CJ Henderson,
who always kept pushing me.

and

To my mother, Barbara Anne Ackley,
who has always looked beyond.

INTRODUCTION

When introducing a collection of short stories, I'm not one to give the reader a preview of each story. They already have their introductions—well-expressed ones at that. Instead, I like to think about the collection as a whole. Danielle's collection, *Transcendence*, is perfectly named for the stories and poems within.

To transcend. "To go beyond the range of normal or merely human experience."

All authors attempt to tell stories to the reader about something bigger than themselves; to share parts of themselves or to impart knowledge or wisdom or experiences. Even the authors who "only" wish to entertain. There is the need to affect the reader, to touch them in some way.

To transcend. "Surpassing the ordinary."

Even when the stories are steeped in mundane trivialities, authors try to bring a new point of view, a new perspective to the ordinary, and to make it extraordinary. Stories are all about going beyond what is and rush forward into what could be. No matter how impossible that might seem. In and of themselves, stories transcend reality by being exactly what they are.

Danielle's collection embodies these two concepts. Each story sets the reality for that world, then has the characters—protagonists and antagonists alike—surpass what is there. Or, to be given the chance to transcend their roles, only for them to deny the opportunity. Even when I, a reader, was shouting at them to do something else.

These stories touched me. They made me think. And, as an author, they inspired me. I can think of no better compliment to give another author. These stories are so good that they make me want to write and to share as well.

I have my favorites, of course. "If I Had the Chance" made me put down the collection so I could think about what I had just read and to think about what I would do if I were also in that position. The poem "Luna" made me smile and to go look at the night sky. "Stoli and Solitude" made me ponder my marriage as I approach seven years with my beloved husband.

The point is, Transcendence is a collection of stories that will affect you. How? I don't know. You and I are different people and different readers. The only thing I am sure of is that you will enjoy this collection and it will touch you. Some of the stories may make you think. Some may make you angry. Some may make you smile. All of them will entertain.

In the end, what more can you ask for in a short story collection?

—Jennifer Brozek
author of *BattleTech: The Nexus Affair*

On "Skippy"

Full disclosure—for a horror writer, I'm a huge chicken. I don't do scary movies, I don't do haunted houses, and there's no way in HELL I go into a mirror maze. So this story about what happens when a haunted house goes rogue pushed a lot of my buttons. It's creepy, atmospheric, and shocking all at once, with a character that you care about from the beginning and an awesome back-and-forth struggle. Go ahead, venture forth into Danielle's lair of terror—there's nothing in there that could possibly hurt you. After all, these things are all make-believe, right? Right?

—John Hartness
author of the *Bubba The Monster Hunter* series

SKIPPY

Kylie's screams shredded the air the way shards of glass cut through cobwebs. She jerked back, her hands shaking violently. Something cool and slimy flew off them and slapped against Don's cheek as he brought his hands up to steady her.

"Eww! Eww! EWWW!"

He didn't say a word, but Don agreed; whatever she'd flicked off her hand now slid down his face and was now heading inside his shirt. One hand came off Kylie's shoulder to intercept it. His fingers rubbed across something the consistency of chilled jelly. Every year the haunted house changed. Whoever designed it this year had gone all-out.

The effort was not lost on his baby sister.

"No! No! I can't do it! I can't! I want to go back." Kylie whimpered. She continued to back up until she pressed tight against his chest. When he didn't move, she slammed herself into him and pushed, as if determination alone would send him the way they had come. Somewhere in the dark ahead of them rose a witch's cackle. Kylie jumped at the sudden sound and renewed her efforts with more force. Her little body crashed against him like a battering ram. He had to brace himself more than once as she pulled away and slammed back over and over. For all her fierceness, he smelt the acrid scent of her fear and responded.

"Shhh...shhhh..." With ten years between their ages, Don was used to soothing his twelve-year-old sister. They shared some link that made him particularly suited for it, a connection beyond the norm. He could not explain except to call it a mental ability. Not telepathy, not empathy, but something that allowed him to influence her. He could not make her do things, but if emotion clouded reason, he could clear it away; kind of like calming by osmosis. It worked best if they were touching, but that was not necessary.

His clean hand came off her shoulder and smoothed down her sandy curls so he could rest his chin on top of her head. As he did so, he brought both arms around her slender shoulders in a sheltering hug. He spoke because she expected it, though it was not what he said out loud that made a difference. "Come on, darlin'. It's okay. We're almost there."

"I want to go back." This time she braced against him and used her muscular legs to push him back. "I want to go back!"

Kylie was nothing if not stubborn. He could hear it in her voice. Intractable, unyielding...she would dig in with both feet all night. Leaning forward to cancel out her nearly successful efforts, he chuckled and rubbed her arms gently.

"Sweetie," Don allowed amusement to edge into his voice. "Think about it, we're over halfway through. If we turn around now you'll just have to go by the creepy stuff all over again."

She remained silent a long moment. He could feel her scalp shift forward. In his mind, he saw the glowering pout so familiar to him. He gave her a little extra squeeze, another mental push. Growling, she slapped at his arms until he let her go.

"Never again! Never again, Donkey-breath!" She whirled as she spit the words at him. As she turned, artificial lightning cracked through the dank 'graveyard' they stood in the middle of. The setting and the spooky glow made her glare downright ghoulish despite the silver tracks of tears glittering on her cheeks. If she weren't so young and his kid sister, Don would have been doing some serious back-pedaling himself. Instead, he smiled.

"Come on, Ky, you say that every year. This was your idea, you know."

Her scowl deepened and her tiny hands curled into hard, little fists. He chuckled and grabbed them before she could bring them into play.

"Hey, find the way out and the caramel apple's on me."

Her fists stayed clenched, but the scowl lost all its heat. Kylie suddenly grinned as if she were six. "A caramel apple and cotton candy," she countered.

Don let go of her hands, held out one of his own, and shook on it. He chuckled and waited patiently as she visibly gathered her courage to move forward. They weren't in any rush. The lady who tore their tickets told them they were the last ones for the night, so it wasn't like anyone was going to come up on them.

Ahead the shrieks and laughter of those who had gone before grew fainter. Time to continue on or they would end up locked in for the night. They moved through darkness and shadow in a quick hustle. Canned shrieks and maniacal laughter kept pace with them, while burning red "eyes" blinked from unexpected places. The occasional denizens of the dungeon leapt out, only to fade back once Kylie screamed. Near the end, the floor beneath the grate they walked on fell away to reveal the illusion of a raging inferno below, as if they were about to plummet straight to hell. Kylie simply clutched his hand a little tighter and plowed through, squealing as low-flying "bats" zipped by.

Finally, the moss-draped exit came into sight. Don barely registered Kylie's gasp as the door clanged shut behind them. He was too busy gulping hard. The exit had not led outside; it led to a hall of mirrors.

He turned to push back through into the haunted house, only to find that there were no handles on this side of the door.

"Wow..." Kylie's tone came out hushed with awe. The wonder in her voice drew him back around. He struggled to force away his own less-eager reaction. For her, Don plastered a smile on his face. A strained grimace reflected back at him a thousand-fold.

Crap. This was not good. If he'd known this was here, he would have given in to Kylie's insistence to go back the other way. Something lurked behind the silver-backed glass, something hungry. Something primal instinct told him to avoid. He'd encountered it once as a child and had avoided mirrored mazes ever since. Hell, he avoided any mirror, if he could.

This time he had no choice; the way out led straight through that perilous maze. For the first time ever Don wished his link with Kylie went both ways. The best she could do was hold his hand, only his ego could not stand the blow of letting her know how freaked he was.

"Oh wow! Will you get a load of this..." Kylie started forward and it was Don's turn to dig in his heels. She turned to look at him, the memory of her own fear quickly fading. The corners of her mouth drew down and her brow furrowed as she grabbed his hand and tugged. "Come on, Don Quixote, face your demons."

Internally, Don flinched. Demons. Apt word. Thousands upon thousands of them stared back at him. Each one wore his face. Literally mirroring his every move. In theory, he held the power over them. After all, what could a reflection do but follow his steps? His forehead immediately filmed over with sweat. He gave in to his need to keep hold of her hand. He had learned long ago that reflections could be more than they seemed.

"Cut it out, Ky."

"Hey, it's just a maze." Her tone softened as she saw through his efforts to remain calm. "Let's go, we'll be through it in no time. I promise, this time I'll protect you."

Reluctantly, he let her draw him forward. He watched the thing with his face, waited for it to make its move. When he looked at it head on, it matched him exactly, over and over in endless repetition. Except for the glimpses he caught from the corner of his eye. Those made him tense. Those expressions and actions did not exactly mirror Don's own.

He continued to let Kylie lead the way. Her reflection stayed true to form, never deviating. She came up against the mirrors and merely pushed away, continuing her search for the pathway out. That was how it should be. The natural order of things.

Don scrupulously avoided the walls of the maze.

Kylie laughed and the sound tinkled off the glass. Hard to believe no less than ten minutes ago she'd been petrified. Don clutched her hand tighter. Without realizing it, his steps slowed. Their arms stretched between them. In the mirrors, his reflection reaching for him. His eyes went wide and he shuddered to a stop.

"Whoa...hello! My arm is attached," Kylie groused. "I'd kinda like it to stay that way. Come on, it's not funny anymore. What's up with you, anyway?"

He could not answer. She gave a tug and he followed. They left the corridor and found themselves in a huge, octagonal chamber with enough space to hold a small dance. The center of the maze.

As they stepped full into the room a sharp click sounded. The lights dimmed even further as the floor slowly rose and tilted like a low, wide top. Another click and a disco ball lowered from the ceiling. The spangled light effect combined with the shifting floor disoriented Don.

Kylie giggled and pulled him into the center of the room. The floor continued to tilt, but not enough to make them fall. She grabbed him by both hands and, with a mischievous grin, she started them spinning. Her laughter rose bright and good. Don's terror ebbed and he told himself not to be silly. The nightmares he had had since childhood were not possible. What he half-remembered from that long-ago time in another hall of mirrors could not be possible.

His sister's joy and his own common sense chased back the demons. He smiled and put effort into spinning them even faster, leaning back, as Kylie did, to increase their momentum. The disco ball picked up speed, the floor tipped steeper. Don added his laughter to his sister's. The faster they went, the more their fingers slipped from each other's grip.

"Oh, shit!" Don reached frantically to strengthen his hold. What were they thinking? He had visions of them flying backward into the glass. Images of shattered, bloody shards flashed in his mind. "No!"

He could not help it. His grip released and they both flew back in opposite directions, Kylie laughing all the way. She was still laughing when they landed. No tinkle of shattered glass followed.

Don hit hard, but not against the mirrored wall, though even with his eyes closed he could tell it was close. For a moment he could not move. When he could, it was only to roll onto his stomach. His body shook in delayed reaction and, in his thoughts, Don thanked the Lord that their stupidity had not had worse consequences. He rested his forehead on the ground and called out to his sister.

"Hey, Ky...you okay?"

"Yeah." Giggles threaded her voice and he heard the faint scraping of denim as she picked herself up. "How about you?"

"Just give me a minute."

Bracing both arms against the floor, Don looked up to see just how close he had come to disaster. He gulped as his hair brushed the wall. He blinked, eyes rising to the mirror. His dazed surface reflection stared back. Something else gleamed beneath it. Fear flooded to the fore. He scrambled to his feet too quickly. His heart clenched hard and he could not get a breath. He swayed and felt himself fall forward.

The mirror was too close. His choices were to brace against the glass, or fall into it. Before he could decide, his hand came up in automatic reflex. Rested against the cool surface, it stabilized his balance in that critical moment. He blinked his eyes and drew a hard breath. Any second he expected his world to end. Nothing happened.

He laughed and the sound had an edge to it. What a complete spaz, letting a silly childhood fear tie him into knots. His forehead came to rest against the mirror. His eyes drifted closed. A moment to relax, to regain his equilibrium, that's all he needed.

That moment was all his reflection needed, as well.

A sharp tingle burned across his skin. Eyes snapping open, Don stared into his nightmares. The gaze that met his own in the mirror was black with hatred, thick with jealousy. Venom whispered through his thoughts. It reminded him of his link with Kylie, only twisted.

'Hello, brother.'

'What the hell!' The thought formed, but he knew he did not voice it out loud. That did not seem to make a difference. Don struggled to pull back, to break contact, but the mirror held him fast, as if his flesh had melded with the glass.

'You've been avoiding me. Time to get a little closer...'

Don had no chance to respond. A shock raced over his skin. Then a second one, deeper still. His body buzzed. He throbbed and ached with the sensation. It felt like two of him fought to occupy his skin. The world darkened and dimmed around him. He tried to scream. It sounded only in the silence of his mind.

'What are you?' He forced the thought past the pain.

'Why, I'm your evil twin.'

Don put every ounce of effort into pulling away. Agony ripped at him. A malicious chuckle tore through his mind as some force yanked him forward. He fought it with everything he had.

'Behave, brother, it's my turn to come out and play.'

'You bastard!'

'Actually, I prefer Skippy.'

Faint and far off, a sound drew Don's attention from the struggle. His heart clenched and a moan shuddered through him.

"Don, you okay?"

No! Kylie! But he could not answer. The demon had silenced him. It took everything he had to fight back.

"Hey, Don Juan, you're scaring me here. You hit your head or something? Or are you just busy making kissy-face with your reflection?"

An evil laugh drowned out whatever else she might have said. Don shrieked as a surge of power washed over him. Intense pain...a tingle across his skin. He fell, his body passing through endless slivers of glass.

He landed hard. There was nothing left but agony and bright light. He forced his way past the torment. Scrambling to his feet, he turned and sought his sister. Panic nearly threw him down again. He saw her through a smoky haze, from every possible angle at once. Already disoriented, Don swayed. He closed his eyes against the sensation. Silence and darkness wrapped him tight. He stood stranded in a vacuum with Kylie trapped outside.

Don's eyes flew open again and he fought to focus through just one view, to be in a single place at once. He stared into Kylie's face, but her gaze did not quite meet his. She smiled at the Don-who-was-not-Don as if nothing had changed. The love and trust in her gaze was tangible as she reached for his hand. For Skippy's hand.

'No! Ky...Ky!' Don frantically tried to make her hear him. 'Sweetie, run! That's not me!' His voice cracked and he pounded on the haze, desperate to shatter it. He fell.

Laughter sounded again in his head, in sharp, shredding jags.

'There's nothing there for you to hit, dear brother, not unless I touch it from this side.'

Skippy's malice rode the twisted link and hit Don hard. In reaction, rage shook him. He ground his teeth against another scream. He would not give the demon more cause to taunt him. Don's focus slipped and he saw his nightmare from a thousand dizzying views. Ky and Skippy were pulling away. Heading for the second half of the maze. Determined, Don followed them.

His every step mirrored Skippy's. At first he fought it, but the drain ate away at him. It stole his thoughts and his will until he could not remember why he fought at all. He was too new to the mirror realm to fight it. That added to Don's fury. Skippy's motions forced Don to follow, to watch, helpless as Kylie scrambled to keep up. The demon ruthlessly dragged her through the maze.

Don gave up on calling out to his sister. The place that trapped him also hedged in his words. Gritting his teeth, he locked his eyes on Kylie. He had to reach her. He thought of the link they shared, tried to sense if it still remained. The effort nearly floored him; would have, if he were not chained to Skippy's motions. His will struggled as if he were encased in thick glass. The mirror realm muffled everything, including the link between him and his sister. He could tell it remained, but only as a mere shadow of itself. He called it. Willed all of his strength into it. Did something he had never done before: used it to make his sister anything but calm. He projected an image at her, one where she fought the grip of a stranger masked by Don's face. He felt, more than saw, as doubt and uncertainty took hold of her. Beginning wisps of fear drifted into her gaze. She no longer scurried to keep up.

Skippy shot Don a venomous look through the mirror's reflection, but did not speak or slow his pace. If anything, his steps grew more urgent. Don roared and whipped his fist through the haze. He knew now what drove his evil twin: the exit. They were nearly out. And once they passed the threshold Don would lose his chance of escape.

'Yes! Yes you will.' Skippy hissed in Don's thoughts. 'Once we go through, you are damned forever.../trapped forever.'

Insanity tinged the demon's laughter. From the look on Kylie's face, she had heard it as well. She stumbled and Skippy jerked her hard to her feet, not even stopping.

Don thought the image at her again, stirring her doubt. He wavered with the effort.

Kylie instantly transformed. Her fear and confusion morphed into a familiar glower. Her free hand fisted and her feet planted firm and would not be budged.

Yes! Don knew his first glimmer of hope since he had been yanked through the glass. 'Come on, honey, come on. Look at him, Kylie. See him! That could never be me.

'Get away, Ky!'

He watched as her gaze went from Skippy, to his reflection, and back again. She could not possibly hear Don, or see him, but did she begin to consciously feel him? Her brow drew down even further and she showed her teeth. Yes!

'That's it. You wouldn't take any of that from me...don't take it from him, Kylie. I love you, sweetie. Just get away.'

Don gathered all his will and focused everything on the thought of his sister getting free, pictured her pulling away. His frustration built as Skippy dragged Kylie closer to the exit. One of the demon's hands reached for the handle, while his other jerked Kylie brutally, drawing her along.

Kylie growled and yanked back, but could not break Skippy's grip. Don watched her yank again, throwing all of her body behind the effort. He continued his pinpoint focus on her, trying to lend her strength. He weakened and his world went several shades darker. He hardly noticed as Kylie slammed backward, dragging her hand from Skippy's. She collided with one of the mirrored panels. A spider's web of cracks fractured the silver-backed surface, the impact point smudged with blood; Kylie slid to the floor. She did not move.

Don cried out and tried to go to her, but he could find no way through the haze. His rage built and he no longer feared the demon. Not when he meant to tear it apart.

He looked up and met Skippy's gaze. As earlier, his reflection showed him fear. This time not his own.

'No! You cannot touch me!' Skippy screamed in Don's mind. 'You cannot pass back. It's my turn!'

Don just stared at him, as if memorizing a face he'd not seen before. He allowed his intentions to shine through. Skippy paled and backed away. Don just smiled an unpleasant smile. He also noticed something he had missed: the haze around him slowly thinned, like smoke escaping through a crack. Sound filtered through the fractured mirror. Calliope music; the hawkers' last cries from beyond the exit door; and Kylie's moan, as she came back to herself.

The smile on Don's face took on a satisfied gleam. The moment he heard his sister's unmuffled moan, he knew. He mentally reached out to her. His suspicions were confirmed: The barrier was breached. The horror on Skippy's face clinched it. Don reached up and placed his hand against the haze, watched it shimmer and deepen to a silver sheen. Skippy scrambled back, colliding with a mirror on the other side.

This time Don purposely eased back his focus. He went from the singular point he'd clung to, to being everywhere at once. The tightness returned as Don stared into the madness of Skippy's haunted eyes. With a thought, he drew the demon to him with an unyielding grip. Again, Don's body held two of him. No agony, this time, but as he pushed through what felt like a stream of warm silk, he heard Skippy's tortured scream as the other fell back through endless slivers of glass.

Don landed hard with his senses still cloaked in a shimmery haze. Avoiding the glass, he pushed himself off the floor. He knelt in place, legs spread wide, until he swayed no more. He raised his eyes to his reflection, braced for a glimpse of Skippy's hatred.

The mirror held nothing of the other. Don's reflection stared back at him from the glass, and it was him alone. Skippy was gone.

Only then did Don edge forward. He pulled Kylie into his lap and wrapped his arms around her. She stirred as he pressed his lips to the top of her head.

"Welcome back," she murmured, her voice faint as she sank into his hug. "Where'd you go?"

Don smiled down at her and whispered back, "You don't want to know, but for busting me out, you get two caramel apples."

DERVISH

spinning
    spiraling
        whirling
dervish
    divinely twirled
        from point to point
  slow a moment
    and you whisper
in my ear
    the secret of
        immortal wisdom
    of standing still
unmoving
    tranquil
        and savoring
  a mercurial world
as it passes
    in frenetic activity

On "The Kindly One"

Within the walls of a women's prison, the only rules that anyone respects are force and fear. For hardened killer Callie, destined to spend the rest of her life here, there's nothing to hope for except to stay at the top of the pile—whatever that takes, even if it means rending asunder the ties of blood. Who dare challenge her?

Danielle Ackley-McPhail tells an uncompromising tale of brutal actions and their terrifying consequences.

—John Grant,
co-author of the *Legends of Lone Wolf* series

Brutally honest and unforgiving, the plot is enthralling and the characters are terrifying. The author's style of writing is keen, to the point, and utterly captivating. Here is one author I will definitely be reading more of.

—Bloody Mary,
Horror Web

THE KINDLY ONE

Guilt, the venom running through humanity's veins,
The cancer eating mankind's soul.
Death, both courted and earned, well fed upon denial.

DUST ROSE IN A ROOSTER'S PLUME ON THE HORIZON LONG BEFORE there was anything to see on the road. Something big was coming in...something bigger than the usual transport bus.

Callie Dupree watched as Warden Schmidt strode across the compound with purpose, his expression twisted into twenty kinds of pissed off. Guards trailed him out the building until three times the normal detail paced the wall, clustered in the towers, and stood positioned around the compound. Each one ran hands unconsciously along the stocks of their rifles or the lengths of their nightsticks. The warden's gaze slid from the crowded Yard to his men. He tensed further when his eyes locked on the approaching dust cloud. He swore as he headed for the main gate. "A bit more ga'damn warning would have been decent."

Near-forgotten in the Yard, the inmates wandered toward the fence that ran along the dead zone between their enclosure and the road that crossed the prison perimeter. They milled in a loose throng, their attention riveted on the goings-on. They gathered as close as they could to the barrier without touching the charged links. For once none of them paid attention to turf or boundaries. Everyone was too caught up in the tension hanging in the air thicker than the desert heat.

The warden lifted a walkie to his lips and handsets squawked all over the compound. Callie edged closer to a nearby guard, trying to hear what was going on. An acrid tang wafted from the young kid in his all-too-new uniform. His dull, dirt-brown hair hung in damp hanks over his forehead and his eyes were black and shocky. He jerked as the warden's voice came hard and flat over the handset. "Weapons at the ready, the Feds are bringin' her in."

Callie's cheek ticked. She carefully worked herself away, watching as the guard cocked his weapon, his hands trembling. She recognized the look on his face—after fifteen years on the inside she'd seen it plenty enough. This one was likely to do something stupid. She was not going to be anywhere within range when that happened. Instead, she worked her way across the yard to Joelle's side.

"Someone new is being brought in. Got half of them wired enough to piss themselves." Callie murmured, her face neutral and her eyes half closed in cultivated boredom. She pushed a length of steel-grey hair behind her ear, revealing ghostly track scars up and down her arm before tucking her thumbs into the waistband of her prison-issue jeans.

"Yeah, and the other half enough to open full bore." Joelle spit in disgust. "They couldn't do this a week from fuckin' now, could they? They're gonna be agitated for months, breathin' down our neck every damn second. I hate the bitch already."

The warning claxon sounded, cutting off further comment. The two women turned with the others, eyes trained on the approaching vehicles. The caravan consisted of a dark, official-looking sedan, followed by a semi, which was then followed by another sedan.

This was not the usual prisoner transfer. Murmurs of speculation buzzed the air like locusts. They cut off a mere moment later. The semi sped up recklessly, weaving the width of the road, the trailer swaying dangerously behind. There was a screech of metal on metal and the squeal of tires skewing sideways on the asphalt as the truck zoomed past the lead sedan, clipping it in passing. There were gasps and yells as the government car peeled off into the sagebrush, smoke pouring from the front end, airbag powder clouding the inside.

Half the guards boiled out of the gatehouses and towers like ants out of a collapsing mound. The rest maintained their posts. All of them had their weapons raised and trained on the semi barreling through the gate. Twenty feet of electrified fence wrapped around the cab, arcing and sparking like Fourth-of-July fireworks. The guards in the truck's path scrambled behind the jersey wall that ran along the asphalt parallel to the security fence. Brakes squealed until the tires smoked thick, black, acrid smoke. At the same time, the engine revved.

Callie was close enough to see the expression on the driver's face. He was paler than chalk and his eyes burned just this side of madness. For a second, she figured he was not going to halt the rig at the inner security gate either. It was almost a disappointment when the truck came to a whiplash stop a few feet before another collision. The second sedan fishtailed to a halt behind it, blocking the breached gate as well as it was able to. Feds poured out the far side and positioned themselves with guns braced on their car as they used it for cover.

The trucker forced his door open against the twisted fence tangled with the front of his truck. The frantic babble drifting out of the compartment sent shivers up Callie's spine. Beside her, Joelle went dead still.

"Damn..." Callie drew the word out long and low, her gut turning over in a hard knot. "Who do they have in the back, Satan's mother or something?"

The guy scrambled from the truck and staggered toward the group behind the barrier. Feds and guards alike barked for him to drop to the ground where he was. He acted as if he did not hear them, listening, as he was, to whatever went on in his head. A second warning rang out, also ignored.

"Oh crap!" Callie yelled. "Down!" About three quarters of the inmates listened, including Joelle. The air exploded with revolver fire and the crack of the guards' rifles. They took the driver down.

It should have ended there, one man on the ground.

There was a strangled moan to Callie's right. She looked up and all she could see was the raised rifle of the young guard she'd noticed earlier, his eyes wide and his knuckles white against the barrel and stock. Boom! Boom! Chi-chink...Boom! Boom! She ducked once more as bullets ricocheted off the metal trailer into the Yard. There was the thud of more bodies hitting the ground. Both men and women screamed; anger, fear, and pain rose in an unholy chorus.

"For chrissake! Hold your fire!" The warden's voice cut through the chaos. "Someone relieve that fool of his weapon!"

Callie lifted her eyes from the dirt and scanned the compound. The Feds were positioning themselves around the truck and driver. Half of the guards had their weapons trained on the semi, a handful pinned the trigger-happy guard to the ground, and the rest were split between tending the wounded and covering the inmates.

Someone whispered, "The sins of the father...madness demands madness."

Callie tried to see who, but no one was near enough that she should have been able to hear them, except for Joelle, and she had not said a word. A shiver traveled from Callie's neck to the tips of her limbs and she looked toward the circle of guards.

The truck driver lay crumpled on the concrete, his blood spreading around him like a flamenco dancer's skirts. He still babbled, though the words grew fainter. "Get outa my head... can't judge me...no...didn't do nothin'...didn't touch...didn't mean nothin'...talkin' ain't illegal...outa my head...shut up!" his dimming gaze flickered back and forth from the truck to the guards huddled around him, his expression frantic and pleading. A final whisper slipped from between his lips. "Save...me."

Across the compound, the young guard twitched where he lay, his expression in a state of constant flux, his sanity in shards. Callie suppressed a shiver and turned her eyes away. She climbed to her feet with utmost caution. Joelle scrambled up next to her. All around them, others stood in stunned silence.

One of the Feds stepped forward. "Warden Schmidt? You need to clear the area."

Behind him, the rest of the government men were securing the zone, dealing with the dead body and the crazed guard, several waited by the trailer's rear doors. The guards were already herding the inmates out of the Yard. Callie trailed back as much as she could get away with, trying to catch a glimpse of whatever monster required an entire, heavy-duty tractor trailer and several car loads of G-men to bring her in.

"Move it!" one of the guards growled. Whack! Callie caught a club across the shoulder. She gritted her teeth and kept silent, but Joelle was still by her side and she had the devil in her eye.

"Bet you hate turnin' that in at the end of the day," Joelle tossed back at the guard in a deceptively causal tone. Her gaze trailed down the length of him. "Must be like castration, seeing as that's more equipment than what you got dangling."

The guard got in a good backhanded slam across her kidneys with the nightstick before another guard stepped in.

"Yo, man," he murmured. "Not with the Feds here."

Callie hauled Joelle away before anyone else decided to take any kind of shot. "What do you think you're playin' at?"

Joelle's gaze was flat and cold, with something else flickering deep behind barriers nearly as good as Callie's own. Somehow Joelle managed to give off the impression of sneering without lifting her lip. She was good at that.

"Hey, he got off your case, didn't he?" She blinked and gave the barest lift of her shoulder.

Callie practically felt a tick mark go down on the negative side of her mental tally of debts owed. Every muscle tensed and she dropped her hand from Joelle's arm. With practiced ease, she invaded Joelle's personal space and captured the young woman's eye from right up closer, leaving no room for misunderstanding. She let her own expression go heavy and hard. "Don't pull that kind of crap again, I take my licks. I haven't fought my way through fifteen years of permanent residence for some young punk like you to make me out as weak in front of anyone. I'm already in for life; you do one more thing that threatens to cut my sentence short and I'll take you out myself."

Joelle went very still. Her jaw twitched and her expression went blank, but her eyes burned. They had a bit of a stare-down that Callie had no trouble holding until Joelle's gaze flickered away. As far as she was concerned, the debt of moments ago had been discharged when Callie gave the girl fair warning.

"Yeah, whatever," Joelle blew her off. "They're heading us to the Mess, Mama. Guess they're dishin' lunch early."

Mama. Callie suppressed a shudder. She might have pushed the kid out twenty-five years before—there was no denying that, to look at Joelle's face—but Callie never played house with her. And still the girl managed to follow in her footsteps. The stupid bitch. No surprise there though, she even had the balls to show up and claim the relation. As if it got her anything on the inside.

Normally, Callie ignored her each time she made any reference to it. Reacting only encouraged her more. Not this time, though.

"Any maternal instincts I had died a long time ago, chicky, right about the time my milk of human kindness dried up. You would do well to keep that in mind. You are nothing to me but a punk stupid enough to try and challenge me."

Wisely, Joelle remain silent. Callie waved her on to the Mess but lingered behind herself. She glanced back down the corridor. The door to the Yard was still open as the last of the guards entered the building. Past their shoulders, she could just make out the Feds hustling their prisoner to Processing. There were two chain-link fences, with great rolls of razor wire coiled at the base of each one, and the dead zone between them, but it was like none of that was there, as if no more than a few feet were between them. Two things she noticed immediately: this one was big and tall...like Guinness World Record tall, and for some reason she was wrapped in an odd, layered cloak that looked like soft, buttery leather.

Callie took in the rest of the woman, weighing what she saw. The matte black hair wafting down her back swayed as if ruffled by a breeze, though the air was dead still, and below the cloak the woman's calves and feet were bare. Perhaps the prison system hadn't had anything large enough to cover them. Or perhaps the behemoth had a nasty disposition to go with that imposing physique and no one dare get close enough to outfit her properly. She was shackled, though, hand and foot. The links were made of steel thick enough that Callie could make them out clearly from where she stood.

Things were about to get interesting.

The new prisoner stopped, forcing the Feds in front to scramble back. They yelled and menaced the prisoner, trying to get her to resume moving forward. To Callie, they seemed like teeny-tiny Chihuahuas snapping at the legs of a Great Dane. The Great Dane ignored them; instead she turned and looked back. Their eyes met. Callie longed to jerk hers away, but the woman's tar-black gaze was inescapable.

Across the distance, the prisoner's head tilted ever so slightly, as if she were listening for something. Her face was both disturbingly devoid of expression and fierce all at once. Her eyes were sharp and assessing, so overt it was grounds for a slap-down on the Block. Callie lifted her chin and allowed her lip to curl. She dared the woman to judge her. So she was big, and whatever she had done, it had both the Feds and the guards as worked up as a prairie dog town with ferret musk on the air, but Callie backed down to no one.

The prisoner nodded, and then turned and walked from sight, followed by the startled Feds, their procession in total disarray.

The mess hall was thick with whispers.

"No prison will have her..."

"...people end up dead..."

"They say she's a monster."

Callie ignored the gossip. Wasn't no one in this place—inmate or guard—what wasn't a monster in some way, and people were always dying...with or without help. She wasn't going to give credence to any talk. If this new one wanted a face-down, Callie would put her in her place; if not, she wasn't worth the speculation. None of them were.

She gathered her tray and the slop they were dishing and turned to her usual spot: A table along the back wall where she could see everything and no one could come at her back. The table was large, heavy, industrial grade, and supposedly bolted to the floor. Over the years, Callie had removed and stripped those bolts, using any tool she could get her hands on to cut off most of the length until only a nub was left to hold the bolt in the hole. When she'd done it, it had mostly been a matter of boredom, and wanting to rebel against the establishment. Besides, tipped over, the table would make a good shield, or even a diversion, if she needed one. The table was hers, an indication of her power.

Some people didn't get that...or maybe they did.

Joelle was already there, sitting in Callie's seat. That girl had to push it; and several other dumb fucks had joined her.

Callie had no problem pushing back. She slid a look to the others at the table, her gaze snapping and her expression deadly flat. Most of them immediately swept up their lunches and cleared away. A couple of the dumber ones hesitated, as if feeling for a shift in power. Callie just smiled and let her breath out in a soft *hmph*. She half closed her lids, looking them each in the eye. Without a word, but with plenty of haste, they abandoned their trays and scurried to other tables.

Once she and Joelle had a measure of privacy, Callie braced her hands on the edges of the tabletop, taking a good grip, her legs braced and her stance wide.

"Perhaps you didn't believe me earlier," she spoke, her eyes as hard as her voice was soft.

Furtive glances shot their way an instant before they were conscientiously ignored. Around them, the conversations climbed several decibels, giving them a bit of cover, of sorts.

It was good to be the Queen. Or the Alpha bitch, anyway. Callie intended to stay in power, and took the necessary steps to strengthen her position.

"You know, you had yourself a baby brother for a while." Callie leaned forward keeping her tone low, so Joelle had to strain to catch her words. "One night I woke up and watched as my man smothered the squalling brat, when he was done I snuck up and killed him before he could do the same to me."

She watched as her careful words formed the proper picture in the space behind Joelle's eyes, watched as they summoned Callie's earlier words: no maternal instinct, no milk of human kindness. The girl went pale and then green, then her lip curled in revulsion. Fear, however, was absent from her gaze.

The fool still did not get it.

Callie shot a look to the side and caught a loyal eye. She jerked her head toward the far side of the room. Moments later, a fight broken out and distracted the guards.

"I believe in taking care of my problems before they take care of me," Callie purred, as she turned her full attention back to Joelle. The girl tensed and looked to either side. More inmates loyal to Callie had drifted in the spaces to either side of the table. Though seemingly not paying attention, they blocked any way of escape.

With a nasty smirk and a massive heave, Callie yanked up hard on the table, popping the bolts out of their holes. Trays clattered to the floor. Joelle gasped. She might have yelled, except Callie rammed the table hard into her chest. There was a thud and a crack, splintering wood from the chair echoed sharply by shattering bone. Joelle glared, teeth clenched against the pain and hatred and defiance barely masked. She hid the fear better, but Callie caught the tremor ripping beneath the dumb bitch's skin. For good measure, Callie yanked the table back and slammed it home again. Then she leaned heavy into the edge and ground it from side to side until it crushed the younger woman a little more.

Joelle gave a strangled gasp, but clearly did not have the air to scream. Her eyes went wide and glassy. Callie ran her gaze appraisingly over her daughter and let a sneer just barely peak her lip. This one was too stupid to live. She could see Joelle's hatred break loose and blossom full in her expression. The girl would have spit if Callie had let up on the steady pressure of the table. She bucked weakly and Callie shoved harder, until blood trickled from the girl's mouth and her eyes turned to hard, lifeless pebbles.

Callie yanked the table back into place and Joelle's body slid silently beneath. Thanks to those loyal to her, none of the guards noticed the goings on. Eventually, someone would say something, but what were they going to do, incarcerate her in the next life too? As long as they did not find the body too soon, any accusations would only be alleged, anyway. Callie kicked the trays on the floor beneath the table with the rest of the trash, and then moved off across the room, the picture of innocence.

It was then that she heard a whisper out of nowhere, drifting on the stale, greasy air of the mess hall. "The sins of the mother...blood calls for blood."

She shrugged it off and turned her back on Joelle. The girl was in no position to attack, and Callie's supremacy remained unchallenged.

Lock Down came early. Callie lay in her cot as the guards shut the Block down for the night. She was too wired to sleep.

Joelle had been discovered at the end of lunch, during head count, as the guards were divvying the inmates up into their work crews. The uproar had been exhilarating, the wrath of the establishment tempered by an edge of fear Callie could not explain, unless it had to do with the newbie and the things everyone was whispering about her. Satisfaction pulled Callie's lips into a seldom-used smile.

Unless someone talked, it didn't seem Callie would ever come under suspicion. She was home free; she'd already made it clear what would happen if anyone said a thing.

She could not sleep. She lay there waiting for dawn to come, her mind buzzing and her body tense with the need to move and do something.

There was a whimper in the semi-darkness, like that of a baby, then a miserable cry. Callie sat up, startled, her pulse racing for some reason she could not explain. She tried to tell herself it was just the excitement of the day working on her nerves, but even as she thought it, the cry escalated into a scream, cut off...smothered by the silence. No one on the Block reacted, not inmate or guard. It was as if the scream had sounded only for Callie's ears.

Suddenly, she could not breathe. She thrashed, slammed her fists into the thin mattress. She felt the weight of the shadows like a pillow over her face, heavier and heavier, anchored by memories...memories of her boy, and of her man. Good memories and bad. Fatal memories. Memories of her daughter. Callie pushed them all away. Her heart hardened. Her face twisted with rage. They meant nothing to her. She stopped being soft long before they drew their last breathes.

Callie forced air into her petrified lungs and unclenched her muscles. With a thought, she cut off the memories. Breathing did not get any easier.

Silence, heavy, thick, and suffocating. Callie fought against it for each breath. She opened her eyes to a shape looming above her, somehow within her cell. The woman's head practically brushed the twelve-foot ceiling. And, with a whoosh, her wings filled the cell.

Callie fought not to cringe, not to strain her eyes to make out the figure before her. It was the newbie, no question. Who else was that big?

Wings? Callie's eyes went wide, the faint light from the corridor backlighting the impossible and imposing wings. "What are you doing here?" she demanded, not even wondering how the bitch broke free of wherever she was being held and ended up in Callie's cell.

"Taking care of business."

"Business? The only business we have in here is to rot." Callie sneered, hiding her growing terror behind toughness.

"No. Your business is to pay."

In an instant, the memories flooded back. Boy babies and girl babies...bruises and needles and punches upside the head... screams...and whimpers...and telling silences. Callie moaned and clenched her fists. She tried to force the memories away once more. Her hands came up to cover her ears and she curled around herself like a baby in the womb. The weight of the world landed on her chest, or at least twelve, tall feet of it did, slamming her flat into the cot, not letting her hide. She looked up into that terrible face. One she had no problem seeing, despite the low light. It was her own face, aside from the eyes. Black, depthless eyes that saw everything with an unforgiving clarity.

Callie gulped and thrashed. Or at least she tried to. That face came closer. The hair framing it caressed her cheek. It did not feel like hair. It did not move like hair. Tiny slivers of fire pierced Callie's skin all over her face and neck. She could feel venom creeping through her veins. Her ears filled with a furious hissing, low and inescapable. No, it did not move like hair. It moved like snakes.

"You...in this place...because you're a monster?"

"No, because you are. Time to pay."

The words were somehow soft and hard and vibrant all at once, the epitome of fury. Callie whimpered. Tears mingled with the blood running in tiny tendrils down her face. She tried to bring her hands up, to push her tormentor away. She could not move and she could not close her eyes. Her gaze was riveted, but she no longer saw the Fury perched on her chest.

The memories came flooding back.

"Save...me," Callie begged to die long before she finally did.

On "If I Had the Chance"

Can destiny be changed? Are we bound by the sorrows of the past? When three-year-old Leana rebels at the tyranny of fate, her beloved grandmother, Ama, gives her a gift like no other. But is such a gift too great a responsibility for so young a child to properly grasp?

If I Had the Chance is a beautiful, bittersweet story of a loving gift gone awry, and a chance to put it all right again.

—L . Jagi Lamplighter
author of the *Prospero's Daughter* trilogy and
The Books of Unexpected Enlightenment series

IF I HAD THE CHANCE

"Destiny cannot be refused."

"Why, Ama?"

"Destiny is set for all, both man and god; we may alter the way in which we reach the end, but nothing more."

Leana's young face drew into a frown, giving form and definition to childhood's vague softness. Her deep, midnight blue eyes crackled with defiance and a glimmer of the formidable woman she would become shadowed her expression. Her reddish-blonde curls did little to soften the look.

"I do not like that, Ama. I want to say what I will do."

Ama laughed and reached out to pull her into a hug. Leana stepped back out of reach, her frown deepening. She loved her Ama, but did not like being laughed at any more than she liked being told what to do. She might only be three, but she most definitely did not like being treated like it.

Even so, the sad look on her grandmother's face was too much for her to stand. Guilt darkened her eyes even further.

"I'm sorry, Ama. So sorry." With the mutability of the very young, her face transformed once more, becoming soft and smooth and loving. She flew into her grandmother's arms and pressed sweet lips against the weathered cheek. "I didn't mean to be mad; I love you so much."

"I love you too, my jewel." Ama returned the hug, pulling Leana onto her lap. "And so, I give you my best advice: never pass up a hug. You never know how many are left to be offered."

Leana looked up into Ama's eyes. The sadness was still there, despite her grandmother's smile. Leana smiled back and slipped her arms around Ama's neck, tucking her head in close beneath the cloud of silver-white hair. The sadness scared her. She did not want to see it anymore. A shiver of unease ran through her and she hugged tighter.

Ama laughed softly in her ear, then pressed a gentle kiss on top her head.

"I tell you what, little one," she whispered. "I shall give you a gift. A very special gift, only first you must make for me a promise."

Leana nuzzled closer and thought a moment. She gave a little nod, too uneasy to speak.

"Okay, the promise is, you must never use what I am to give you for me. It is not allowed. Will you promise that?"

A shiver ran across Leana's skin. She was cold and clung to Ama's warmth. She did not want to answer. She was afraid to, though she had no idea why.

"Well?" Ama asked as she wrapped her arms tighter around Leana. "I must hear your answer before I can give you the gift."

"Yes," Leana whispered softly, hardly more than a breath against her grandmother's neck. "Yes, I promise."

Ama gripped Leana's arms and set her back far enough that they could see one another's eyes. "This is my gift to you: the power to undo one wrong in life."

Leana's head tilted slightly to the side in the way of children and animals. "What do you mean?"

"When Destiny reaches out to draw you that final step, you can look back down the path behind you at all you have seen across the years and make something right that went wrong. In that final moment, you get to decide.

"Do you accept my gift?"

Something Leana would much later recognize as foreboding sent ripples throughout her tiny frame. She looked down at the steady hands holding her shoulders at arms' length. They seemed to glow through thin skin, frail and fleeting. Leana lifted solemn eyes to her grandmother. She wanted to say no. She wanted to reach out with her little-girl hands and hold on tight. But Ama would not let her. The warning was there in her eyes.

A tear ran along the outer curve of Leana's cheek. It was hard to smile, but she did, and instead of clutching for what slipped away, she ran her fingers along the soft satin of her grandmother's arm. She did not speak; she could not. Just a nod of her head and Ama drew her close again, loving arms closed tight and soft lips pressed against her forehead in a fierce kiss. The spot burned long after the lips lifted away. They sat that way a while, Leana silent and Ama humming their little song. The one she always used to comfort.

"Okay, off with you. Ama is tired now."

"Can...can I stay with you?"

"No, my jewel, go play quietly, while I rest."

Leana went as she was told, but she did not play. She sat in the window seat staring out at her Ama's beloved garden. She did not see the flowers though, all she saw was Ama the way she looked as Leana left the room: old and faded, with the glow of moments before gone out of her. Streams of silent tears slowly shaped Leana's face.

"Do you remember my Ama, Cam?"

"What kind of question is that? Of course, I remember her."

She could see Cameron scowling. Knew without doubt the thought running through his head; that she must wonder how senile he grew. That was not it at all though.

"It was so very long ago. And we were so young. I wonder how well I really remember her. How well I knew her. I guess I'll find out soon."

"Oh, for Pete's sake!"

Cameron had thick, bushy eyebrows the color and texture of a Schnauzer's coat, liberally laced with wiry guard hairs. He frowned so deep the brows themselves nearly formed a solid bar, barely dipping in the middle. Fear hid beneath that fierce façade; deep in his eyes, where only Leana could recognize it.

"Hold my hand a while, Cam?" She would not meet his gaze as she asked. She had no right to make his eyes shimmer with unshed tears, then force him to sit here and swallow them back. Only she couldn't not ask. How unfair of her to play on his emotions. She knew he would never leave her alone. She wished she could say the same herself.

"Why did you never marry, Cameron?" Again, the scowl, even deeper this time. Again, no answer. Leana ignored his silence, as she always did. "I will miss you when I'm gone, my friend. It saddens me that there is no one to hold your hand when I must leave you."

"Don't need no one fussin' over me, trying to hold my hand. Besides, you aren't going anywhere, except to Vegas with me once they let you out."

Leana laughed. It was dry and airless, worn away by time and pain. It robbed her of her breath and sharpened the moist glimmer in Cameron's eyes. His grip on her hand tightened and she fought not to wince, not to give him a reason to draw away. With his free hand, he poured her a glass of water, held it to her lips with such practiced precision, allowing her no more than gentle sips, lest she choke even more. It saddened her how proficient he'd grown. He'd suffered with her so long.

She was hiding in the hamper. She did not want to. It was hot and tight and smelled funny. It had not been her first choice, but they had found her everywhere else. Leana buried her face deeper in the sheets that still held Ama's scent. She cried and thought of her gift and cried some more. Her face screwed into a scowl and she bit the sheets to keep her sobs silent. They would find her again. They would find her and drag her back to be fussed over and bothered by people she mostly did not even know.

Leana did not want to be fussed over. She wanted Ama back. She wanted to use her gift to bring Ama back. That was why she cried, more than anything. She had promised Ama she would not use it on her. It was a stupid promise. Just the thought of it made Leana hurt real bad inside. She loved Ama so much she just had to break it; but also because she loved her grandmother, she could not.

This time she screamed into the sheet. Her tiny hands fisted into the fabric until her fingers hurt. She could not hold back any longer. She trembled. Her soft sobs rose in a wail and her throat threatened to close with the tears. Her eyes already had; they had gone sticky and swollen and gravelly with a long afternoon of crying.

That was why she did not hear him.

The wicker top of the hamper flipped up, startling her. Leana gulped back her sobs, her breath catching with each one until she hiccupped. Standing over her was a boy, tall and thin, with dark, dark hair and eyes the color of honey, like the kind deep in the comb Uncle Sid had let her try right from the hive. The boy had to be at least six, or maybe older. Maybe even ten. Leana could not be sure; she did not know him. She scrubbed her face hard against the sheets and scowled up at him.

"G-go away."

He looked at her a moment, his eyes sad. She thought he was going to listen. Instead he squatted down next to her and shook his head. "I can't."

Leana canted her head to the side and frowned at him. His response confused her. Not 'no'. Not 'why?'. Not even 'make me'. Just a quiet 'I can't'. None of her cousins had answered like that. Certainly, none of the adults had. What did he mean, he couldn't?

"Why not?"

He smiled, and that too was sad.

"I promised."

"Promised what?"

"I promised Ama I would stay with you, take care of you."

Leana shrieked and launched herself at the strange boy, tumbling the hamper and its contents to the floor. Her teeth and nails and hard little shoes all came into play.

"No! She's my Ama, not yours! You don't never get to call her Ama! I don't care what you promised. You go away. You go away right now! No one's going to steal my Ama."

She sobbed out that last. The boy fell back until he sat on the laundry floor. He did not fight her. He did not try and get away. Instead he wrapped his long, thin arms around her and wrestled her around until she faced away from him. She bit and tore at the parts of him she could reach. Fought and kicked and bucked with everything she had, until she had no more. Still, he held her, rocking back and forth and humming into her hair.

Leana drew a quavering breath. She looked down at her hands. They were spotted with blood, as was her dress. So were the boy's arms. Her jaw trembled. Silent tears ran down her cheeks. There was no strength left for more. She leaned back and nestled beneath the boy's chin, her hand trying to sooth away the hurt she had caused. As she calmed, she began to hear what he hummed. It was Ama's comfort song.

The boy's arms loosened, but did not let go. Leana squirmed around until she could hug him. She was no longer angry. Whoever this boy was, Ama had loved him too. Ama had comforted him the way she used to comfort Leana. Now, he did it for her. In a way, it was like having a little bit of Ama back.

"What's your name?"

"Cameron Diddle."

Any other time, the name would have made Leana giggle. Now she just remained solemn as she spoke. "Will you make for me a promise, Cameron?"

He was silent a moment, hesitant. Promises were not made lightly. Ama had taught Leana that, and she suspected Cameron had learned it from her as well.

"What is the promise?" he asked cautiously.

"If I let you stay, will you tell me about you and my Ama whenever I want?"

Cameron smiled down at her and leaned a little boy's kiss on her head. "Yeah, I promise."

In the dark laundry room, hidden away from the adult mourners, Leana huddled in Ama's sheets and let Cameron become her friend.

Panic chased away the edge of sleep. Leana blinked, struggled to focus. One arm would not respond. The other was held fast. She willed her arm to move so that she might raise herself up. It stubbornly refused. There was not enough air to moan or call out. Her chest was too heavy; she had no strength to force it up and down for any kind of breathing. She wheezed and tried to free her hand. The more coherent she became the more frantically she fought.

"Hey," Cam's head rose up from the edge of the bed by her hip. "Hey... enough of that; you'll pull out the IVs."

The IVs. Leana blinked furiously and tried to make sense of his sleep-gruff words. She had needles in her arm. Saline and monitors and such. She tugged her other hand and found it now free, Cameron having let go on seeing her distress.

Leana gave him a wan smile and arched herself as best as she was able, trying to open her airway to gain some amount of breath. It was like her chest had hardened to stone, and she was smothering beneath it. Cameron clucked his tongue and shifted by her side. Beneath her, the bed whirred. Slowly she rose higher until she did not have to fight to inhale.

Relieved, Leana closed her eyes and savored the sensation.

"Thank you, Cameron."

"It's getting harder."

She did not ask what. For her, there were so many things that applied. For Cameron, there was only one: watching her suffering. It was not his choice, though. It was Leana's destiny. She had made a promise and gained a gift eighty years ago. She could not rest until she had satisfied both.

"My notebooks."

"Forget the damn notebooks!" Cameron's voice was tight and angry. She could feel as he clenched his fist in her blankets. Reaching up, she brushed his cheek. Surprisingly, it was wet. She opened her eyes and forced herself to look on his pain, to respect it, even if she could not give into it.

"My notebooks, dear heart," she murmured. "From this, you cannot protect me."

He cursed again, low enough that she could not make it out, but with enough passion that she felt it. A sigh escaped her. She brushed her fingers across the back of his hand; the best she could manage for a hug, these days.

"Please, Cam, for me."

Her friend swallowed hard. Made an effort to compose himself. With a sigh of his own, Cameron pushed off from his chair and went to the closet. Inside was box after box of tattered, spiral-bound notebooks. Exactly eighty years' worth, though some had been written long after the events in them took place. He pulled out one at random and returned to her bedside.

"One notebook, from which I will do the reading, and that only once you make me a promise to drink all the lovely shake the nurse has brought you."

Leana made a face. Lovely shake indeed. The thing was surely as vile as all those that had come before it. Protein gobbledy-gook...it was an offense to call such a thing a shake. Still, she nodded in agreement and settled back against the pillows, her eyes trailed on the ceiling and her attention completely focused on his rich, deep voice as Cameron read aloud from her journal.

April 16, 2005: Another women's shelter closed its doors forever today. Lack of funding, lack of volunteers, lack of support from the community. A great and lasting wrong.

Leana finished the entry she was working on and put down her pen. She caught her lip between her teeth and sat back in her chair. Her dress hissed as she shifted, its heavy length sliding across her legs to puddle on the floor. She glanced at the clock and wondered if she had time to read one more section of the paper. No. Not unless she wanted Cam to drag her from her room and carry her downstairs over his shoulder. Her fifteen-year-old mind toyed with the semi-appealing concept.

If she thought she could get away with it—without making him angry in the process—she probably would continue reading until Cameron came to fetch her, as he threatened. But no. At twenty-one, her friend was way too serious-minded to welcome her antics.

There was a tap on the door. Perplexed, Leana glanced at the clock once more. Dirk was not due for an hour. Dirk. Leana grimaced. He was nice enough, but not the boy she wanted to be waiting for. Still, he was the one who asked her to the cotillion and, because Cameron would not let her beg off another dance, Leana had finally accepted.

Another tap interrupted her thoughts.

She turned toward the door, not sure if she really wanted to open it. Anyone she knew was bound to laugh at her in this getup. She felt ridiculous.

Again, the tapping at the door.

"Come in." Leana forced the words past her uncertainty. She kept her eyes on the floor and sat there twisting her ankle back and forth until all she heard was the rustle of her skirt. She listened to that for many seconds, expecting any moment for the person at the door to speak. She moved her gaze forward until she was looking at the floor by the open door. A pair of cross-trainers stood just past the threshold. They did not belong to her brother, Jason. Startled, she lifted her eyes. It was Cameron and the intense look darkening his eyes was one she had never seen before. It left her confused and hopeful all at once.

With a little gasp, Leana turned back to her newspaper. "Well, are you coming in?" she called over her shoulder. Cam was silent a long moment. She forced herself to read the article in front of her, rather than turn to meet that look again.

"I don't know that I should," he finally answered. "It wouldn't be proper."

That startled her enough that she turned to face him, frowning with compounded confusion. "Cam, you have been in my room more times than even my mother has."

"Yeah, but I just this moment realized you've turned into a young lady...no longer the brat I had to come drag from her den."

His teasing words wiped away the intensity. His amber eyes sparkled like warm honey once more.

"Now put away that damn newspaper and finish getting ready."

Leana scowled and pulled her paper closer. "I am ready."

"Half-ready, maybe."

"But...." She could not finish. She was too embarrassed.

"But?" Cameron's voice was kind but firm as he prompted her.

She flushed deeper and started her ankle twisting again. What she knew about hair and makeup would fill less than a column inch of newsprint. Cam cleared his throat and she glared up at him before once again looking away.

"I don't know what to do, and Mom got called in to work before I got home from school. She won't be home until nine."

He tsked. "I told you to read something besides school books and newspapers. What happened to those fashion magazines your cousin Tammy sent you weeks ago?"

Leana's eyes darted toward the heap of glossy pages haphazardly piled beneath her desk. She bit her lip again. She'd tried to make sense of the fashion tips, but it was hopeless. Admitting that failure, though, was not to be considered.

"I had more important things to read."

Cameron grimaced and sent a dark look toward her current notebook. "That is debatable, but I'm not going to argue with you.

"You want some help?"

Leana looked at him in shock. He could not possibly....

Obviously knowing what was going through her thoughts, Cameron cocked his hips and pursed his lips just like Ms. Watson next door when she felt most unappreciated. Leana grinned. She could not help it. No matter how desperate she felt, Cameron would make it all right. She did not know how, but she had no doubt.

He dropped the prissy expression and gave her a soft smile. "Joan is waiting downstairs; all I have to do is give her a shout."

Leana's heart sank at his words and she had to work to hide her disappointment. Joan. She liked to pretend Joan did not exist. She could not fault the older girl for seeing something in Cameron, but it was really inexcusable the way she dominated his time. Leana barely got to see him anymore. But Cameron seemed happy, and he was here when she needed help. Still, she thought she might hate Joan and her place in Cameron's life, so much more important than her own it seemed. Leana's heart broke just a little.

She smiled and looked down so he couldn't see the conflicting emotion in her eyes. She sent Cameron back down the hall with a slight nod. When he was gone, she flipped open her notebook and turned to the next headline. Really, she was better off not caring—about Cameron, or anyone, for that matter. She had thirteen more years of past wrongs to catch up on, plus a notebook for this year to keep up to date. This foolishness would only distract her from her destiny.

Bright sunlight invaded the room through a wrinkle-thin gap in the heavy curtain. She flinched away from the glare across her face.

She must have made a sound. There was a rustle across the room, followed by a grunt. She could hear someone moving toward the window. The faint scent of Brut told her it was Cameron. She heard the shifting of the curtains on their track as the sunlight was banished from her room. She slowly opened her eyes to the soft glow of a desk lamp across the room. She had a moment to notice her notebooks were piled around it. Though he made it clear on a multitude of occasions that he would gladly use those notebooks for kindling, Cam had obviously been sorting through each one for her. Oh, Cam, she thought as he made his way to her side. You are too good to me.

His fingertips brush her cheek. She sighed and turned her face into his touch. "How you doin', kid?"

Leana almost managed a smile. "Okay."

"Can I get you anything?"

"No. Thank you for closing the drape."

Cameron hmphed and she knew she was not fooling him. They were both too aware she had caught him studying her books.

"So, do you have anything to tell me?" Her eyes slid to the mounds across the room, making her meaning more than clear.

"Yes," Cameron answered after a taut silence, taking her hand gently in his own grip. "I dare say I pretty much hate Ama by now."

Leana gasped and tried to pull her hand away. She had not the strength for it, though. She glared at him, hurt and confused. She could not speak, but that hardly mattered, as he did not give her a chance to. His words hit her like stone after cast stone.

"What was she thinking to do this to you? You've been on this planet for over eighty years, yet you've barely lived at all," Cameron's gravelly voice was deep and thick with emotion. "For the love of Mike! You weren't put here to be an observer! To wait for just one moment to make a difference."

The weight of his words crushed down upon Leana. Tears of shame balanced on her lashes. They flooded the dry riverbeds of her wrinkled skin the moment her eyes drifted closed, unable to bear the anguish on Cam's face. Her breath was shallow and the machine beside her bed picked up the pace of its steady beeping.

"Ah! What the hell is wrong with me?" Cameron's soft swearing followed Leana as she drifted back to sleep, too emotionally and physically worn out to stop herself. She was starting to fade when she heard him whisper, "Forgive me...please forgive me, dear heart.

"But how many little wrongs could you have undone if you hadn't just watched your whole life for the big one?" Cameron barely breathed the words. Leana only heard them because his head bowed over her pillow.

She was almost out when he spoke again, though she wondered if she did not imagine what he said next.

"How many we could have fought together if you'd just let me a little closer, if you let me love you the way I've always wanted to?"

Leana's heart broke at the whisper of his words. He was right and she had been so very wrong. In a wash of fatal agony, she knew what she must do.

Leana woke with a cry on her lips and her breath wheezing in her chest. Her left hand trembled where it was fisted in the blanket, her right outright shook, raised in the air as if she were grabbing for something her heart was desperate to have.

She'd dreamt she'd died. The vision of Cameron's devastated face still etched upon her memory, fresh and raw. Beside her, the monitors echoed her strain.

"Cam...Cameron, come here...please." She could hear the faintness of her failing voice, could hear the urgency she was too numb to feel.

There was silence, followed by the barest breath of a sigh. Such an eloquent sound. Tears trickled down her face, tightening skin already taut with illness. She hated causing him such pain.

"Ama..." The voice was Cameron at his most gentle. The voice he used when what he must say would hurt her, though it pained him to do so. But he really was confused. She was Leana, not Ama.

The shadow figure sat forward. Puzzlement swept over her. Cameron met her gaze, love and sorrow mingled in his eyes...but it was a Cameron no older than twenty. She peered closer, her hand reaching out to caress that still-smooth cheek. So soft...it was impossible. His eyes teared at her touch and she felt her own go wide. His eyes were not the color of warm honey; they were deep, dark blue, like her own. He continued speaking and she had to force herself to focus on his words.

"It's Kyle, Ama. Grandpa Cameron passed, last year."

As the young man...her grandson spoke, his words tore Leana in many ways. The grief and outrage she felt conflicted with the wonder and joy. Nowhere among the flood of emotions was there anything resembling objectivity. The resulting turmoil played across her face.

Kyle leaned forward, the concern in his expression echoing so many memories of his grandfather. Leana smiled through her tears.

"No, Ama, please don't cry, don't be sad. Grandpa wouldn't like it!" Kyle spoke in a firm but gentle tone and again she was reminded even more so of Cameron. She managed to stem the tears, but feared sadness still colored her smile.

"I'm okay, love, truly...just...just a bit confused, is all," Leana's energy drained away with her words until the smile was no more than hinted at in the slight uplift at the corners of her mouth. "I'm just muddled by sleep, is all."

Kyle smiled back and gently smoothed her hair away from her face. "It's okay, don't worry about it.

"Hey...I know...how about we look at one of your notebooks?" From somewhere beside the bed he drew up a familiar spiral-bound notebook. His eyes were shiny with unshed tears, but he looked pleased, as if what he offered was a treat.

Leana frowned. Notebooks...but...hadn't she...her gift... surely... Despair crept into her heart, keeping pace with the confusion tightening her face. Beside her the intricate tangle of medical monitors stepped up the urgency of the sounds she had become so used to.

She had thought it was over. That she was done with the gift she had managed to turn into a curse. She so wanted to have done with it! But responsibility beckoned, and, as she struggled to bring herself back under control, she could see she had badly frightened her grandson.

"Maybe you should rest, instead," he murmured, fear darkening his gaze further.

"No! No..." She fought to keep her voice calm and even. "Please, let's look." Leana tried to pat the bed beside her.

Kyle smiled his grandfather's smile and carefully perched himself at her side. He brushed a kiss across her chilled brow and placed the well-worn notebook in her lap before sliding his arm behind her shoulders. He held her as if she was the grandchild, but she did not complain. Instead, she drew upon his strength, as she had upon Cameron's so many times before. Fortified, her hand trembled only slightly as she reached out and flipped the cover open.

She nearly sobbed as her eyes focused on her own neat, precise handwriting. She soaked in the words and all they meant.

"Read it to me, Ama...please?"

Leana felt a sudden sense of the familiar. Kyle's words echoed in her mind in a multitude of voices, all his, from boy to man, all of them endlessly hopeful. She smiled and cleared her throat. Before she could ask, he held a glass of water to her lips. She drank and leaned her head a moment against his shoulder before reaching out and feathering the aged pages, letting them fall at random before she began to read.

"April 16, 2005: Cam and I helped at the woman's shelter today. So many scarred souls, so much pain and suffering. Mom didn't want me to go, said it was too much for a young girl to cope with, but Cameron made it okay with her. She was right, it was hard, but we made a difference..." Leana's voice wavered slightly, not from weariness, but from joy. She finished the passage and then feathered the pages once more. It was an unconscious act, but so familiar, so right, Leana smiled and looked up at Kyle. He shared her smile and his eyes darted to the pages with barely contained eagerness, startling a laugh from her.

"Fine...fine...pick one."

Kyle drew the book toward him and without pretext flipped to the last page. Rather than return the notebook, he held it for her.

"October 11, 2010: Today is our wedding day. So many wrongs in this world we must combat, but Cameron and I take today for ourselves, to celebrate something supremely and utterly right. I find that as I prepare to meet him at the altar, I must thank my Ama in my h-heart," Leana stumbled as emotion choked her. It was a moment before she could go on. Kyle gave her shoulder a squeeze and carefully leaned his head against hers. She composed herself enough to go on. "Cameron is the most precious gift she ever gave to me."

Closing the notebook, she quietly cried in her grandson's arms, tears so joyous her heart ached with them. She closed her eyes and relaxed against Kyle, soaking in his love, feeling his pain. She was so tired. It was so much effort to think...to breath. As she lay there the pages of all her notebooks turned in her mind, each page known to her heart, followed by the images, emotions, and sensations garnered over eighty plus years of living, and living well.

She knew all that had passed, but it was in a way second-hand. That angered her, to have righted things only to remain where she had been, with only the comfort of memories to know she had done it. Rage swept through her until the roar of it drowned out all other sound. Her body protested, heart clutching and lungs gasping for breath. Arms circled her in an echo of that day long, long past when a young boy restrained a child's tantrum.

Leana sobbed at that memory and this moment. Cameron... oh Cameron, why couldn't you make it just a little longer? You promised to look after me, why did you leave me to face this alone? Even as she thought the recrimination, guilt overwhelmed her.

"Ama?! Ama! What's wrong? Nurse!"

As lost as she had been in bitterness, her mind registered the faint, but frantic cries of her grandson, laced with the alarming tones of the monitors. Shame washed over her. What a way to repay the precious gift of remembrance he had given her when he had placed that notebook in her hands. Was she really no better than the three-year-old she had been when she and Cameron first met?

She tried to force her body to calm, to still, and to stop her heart from straining. But she was weak and did not have the strength for it. She cried with frustration and feebly clutched at Kyle's hand.

"No! No..." Kyle's voice cracked. Leana knew she should have felt him clutch her tighter, but it was as if the world that still held him was loosening its grip upon her.

Help me, Cameron, please help me.

A humming filled her ears and the ghost of a kiss brushed her brow. Immediately, the tension drained away, taking her remaining strength with it. Leana would have smiled, only she was too weary. She recognized the hum: Ama's comfort song.

There was no doubt in her as to who hummed. The pain, heartache, and bitterness faded. She turned her head toward the sound, daring to hope, daring to foster her bittersweet happiness. She let the weariness fall away and turned toward where love waited for her.

BELOVED...

You are not gone from us
Death but hides you
From our sight
We've only to turn
To the warmth of our hearts
And the joy of a memory
To feel your gentle hand
Upon our shoulder
To hear your laughter
Rumble by our ear
To catch the glimmer
Of mischief
Ever-present in your eye

Beloved
You are not gone from us
Such cannot be
With love and life
So intertwined

Beloved
You are not gone from us
You wait beside God's feet
For us to come close by
You wait to tell him
These, they love me well
These, they mourn me
These, they are my beloved
As I am theirs
You whisper in His ear
What you would say to us:

Beloved
I am not gone from you...
I love you well

THE MISSES MOIRAI

I FELT LIKE A CONTAMINANT IN THE PURITY OF NIGHT.

Shivers wracked my body, setting off a hundred aches and pains. I bit back a sob. My abused fingertips tingled as I scratched tentatively at the bright blue door in front of me.

It was late, very late. I should not be here. I backed away slowly, but my heel slipped on the loose gravel lining the sisters' walk. I bit off a pained cry as my already battered knee twinged violently in protest.

My breath quavered. What should I do? I could not go back home tonight. It was not safe. But I was only sixteen, so neither was walking around until morning. There was a 24-hour diner on the far side of town, though.

I groaned at the thought of that dump. The coffee always tasted scorched and the cocoa was more chocolate-colored water than anything else. Just the thought of their food nauseated me. Still, it was a safe place to kill the hours between now and dawn. I could always get a Coke.

I turned and carefully made my way back down the walk, my body protesting as the late-night autumn chill stiffened every ache. The gate creaked as I pushed it open. I flinched. Shooting a panicked glance at the door, I nearly screamed. Intense grey eyes stared back.

"Child, why do you turn away?"

Miss Clo, the eldest of the Misses Moirai, stood in the arch of the front door, a skein of variegated yarn in shades of black and blue dangling from her hand.

Did they never sleep? I had yet to visit when they were not deep in some weaving project. It appeared that tonight, despite the late hour, was no different.

"Come back, my girl," Miss Clo beckoned with a gentle smile on her well-worn face. "Sis is about to pour some chocolate."

Chocolate! My mouth instantly watered. The only similarity between the diner's chocolate and the sisters' was the name. I longed for the caress of their thick, rich cocoa on my tongue, the kind they always seemed to have simmering on their old-fashioned stove. Awkwardly, I stumbled, but made it back to the door quicker than I had made it to the gate. The chocolate called to me. The warmth of the parlor called to me, as did the sisters themselves. I needed their comfort.

I watched Miss Clo's expression alter swiftly as I came into the light spilling through the open door. Though I knew her anger was not aimed toward me, I wanted to hunch away from that glare. She did not, however, look surprised.

"That beast..." she began. Her tone sounded as hard as her expression, but it softened and I felt myself relax ever so slightly. "No...it's nothing you need to hear. It's cocoa for you, and perhaps a bit of a fire to warm your toes."

I felt as if I must offer some kind of explanation. But I could not bring myself to tell her that since Mum had gone away, my father had turned into a monster with a familiar face. I would have to make something up.

My tongue betrayed me before I could. "He was thrown out of the pub before he got in his nightly fight," I heard myself murmur.

I blushed at the unintended admission, but Miss Clo merely stepped to the side and drew me in with a comforting arm laid lightly across my shoulders. With care, she led me to the soft cushions of the plaid divan closest to the crackling fire.

"Sis...Posie...look who I found scratching at our door," Miss Clo called out through the house to her sisters as she shifted aside one of the many projects the three of them always seemed to be working on. I sighed as I sank into the overstuffed paisley pillows behind me and allowed the room to add to the aura of comfort enveloping me.

Miss Posie came in clucking from the adjoining room. She laid one of the ever-present afghans across my lap. The blanket wrapped tight about me like a cuddle in my Mum's arms. So much so that I drew its soft folds higher and snuggled most of me beneath it. I truly felt as if my mother hugged me back…wistful thinking on my part. Mum was gone and, though I needed her more now than I had any day since she had left, it was foolish to believe she would all of a sudden appear to comfort and keep me safe. Still, I imagined I smelt the scent of her perfume, a special blend she used to mix herself. When my eyes opened I found Miss Posie watching me. Her gaze seemed both oddly moist and contrastingly grim. She grimaced as she took in the fresh, livid bruise not quite hidden by my bobbed hair. Her lips pressed thin. "Well then, let me just go see what's keeping the drinks." Before stepping back, she brushed the barest of kisses across my forehead.

"Oh my! He certainly did a job, didn't he?"

Startled, I jerked around, dragging myself from the edge of sleep. In the door stood the third sister, Miss Sis. She carried a quirky, antique tray bearing three delicate tea cups and one large mug. I marveled that the rich, decadent aroma of the cocoa they contained had not penetrated my haze sooner. I smiled ruefully and reached up with hands that shook slightly with fatigue. She promptly handed me the mug and did not back away until I brought the rim to my mouth and drank deeply. I licked marshmallow foam from my upper lip and contentment settled deep. There was nothing like the sisters' cocoa. It made the whole world seem to come about right.

"There's the girl," Miss Sis murmured in soft, soothing tones as she set down the tray still bearing the sisters' cups. Her now-empty hand reached out to stroke my hair. I often imagined that was how it felt to have an aunt…or even a grandmother.

"I would have thought he'd learned his lesson the first time."

I sensed a frigid edge to Miss Clo's cryptic words, as she too re-entered the room. She crossed to the divan and settled next to me. Miss Posie glided in and sat on the couch across from us, beside Sis.

There was a long silence as we sipped our cocoa. The combined presence of all three sisters both comforted and intimidated me. I savored my drink and told myself not to stare back but could not help but squirm under their scrutiny. "What?"

They gave one another knowing looks and their heads slowly nodded. "We have to tell her."

"Tell me what?!"

Three identical, time-etched faces turned toward me. Three sets of eyes—grey, green, and blue—anchored me to the cushions.

A sense of the inevitable loomed over me, waking a kernel of fear. It was not a feeling I ever would have associated with the Misses. Of course, there was a time where I never would have believed my father would raise his hand to me, either.

Leaning forward, I carefully placed my half-empty mug on the table. The cocoa sat heavy in my stomach. I would not have thought it possible, but the silence intensified as I warily looked from one woman to the others.

"Tonight is a night of choices," Miss Clo began, her deep voice rumbling in the silence. I shifted sideways, the better to look into her face. And if it moved me ever so subtly further away, well I was comfortable with that.

"The path you choose," Miss Sis continued for her, "will determine the means of your fate."

Miss Posie finished, "But whatever you choose, in this case your fate remains the same: all paths lead to death."

The shakes hit me as numbness wrapped my mind. A disorienting flash of my father's enraged face filled my thoughts and my breath came quicker, my heartbeat banging like war drums in my ears. My hands fisted. I stood quickly and stepped away from them, placing the divan between us. Daddy had taken me by surprise; these women would not.

"That will be enough, Aisa!"

It was hard to say which sister spoke...like it mattered. But the use of my given name—something they rarely, if ever, did— that threw me.

"As if we would ever harm you! Sit down. We speak of destiny." Miss Clo's words confused me. I felt ashamed and doubtful all at once. I sat anyway. After sixteen years, obedience was ingrained. Still, I perched only on the edge of the cushion and nearly vibrated with conflicting tension.

"Know you Greek mythology?"

Miss Sis's question took me by surprise. I was still focused on her sister. I shook my head slowly.

"Three women were born of the gods," Miss Sis went on, "with such power that even the gods themselves must answer to them. They were known as the Fates...the Moirai. They were more powerful than Zeus, their father, for they held even his fate in their hands.

"They were called the weavers of destiny: Clotho, to select the threads of fate; Lachesis, to measure their length; and Atropos, to sever them at the appointed hour."

Clotho...Lachesis...Atropos.... My eyes traveled from one to the other of the sisters. Clo...Sis...Posie.... Coincidence or delusion? Either option seemed more reasonable than accepting this was real. But then I noticed the weary melancholy lurking deep in Posie's gaze. Though the youngest, her eyes seemed the most ancient, the most care-worn.

I shuddered. The tension won out. Like a greyhound after the mechanical rabbit, I shot off the couch. I made it halfway across the room before I found my way obstructed. Those I had left behind me appeared side by side in front of the door.

Miss Clo sighed and shook her head as she locked my gaze and would not release it. "If you will not listen," she said, "we must show you."

The world swirled around me. There was no up or down. I felt pulled in all directions and then none. The darkness remained absolute. I swayed a moment and the spots before my eyes re-solved into a distant neon sign.

Dad must have knocked me around harder than I'd thought. I struggled to focus on the diner just up the road; close enough to see, but far enough away to draw a sigh. Chocolate-colored water began to sound good.

My knee throbbed, threatening to collapse with each step. The other bruises pulsed in jarring contrast. A few hundred more yards and I could rest. I locked my gaze on the sign and all else faded away in the night.

Well...all, except one sound. A rumble grew in the distance. An engine revving with the sound of a manual transmission run hard. Distant high beams lit the road in front of me. I shrank back to the shoulder. The headlights dipped and bobbed erratically from side to side. The rumble became a roar until I smelled scorched rubber on the air. I backed as far as I could into the dense thicket, gut clenching as the sports car's halogens pinned me. Futilely, I braced myself, praying I was far enough back from the road. Knowing I was not...

Even expecting it, I was not ready for the impact as the right front fender slammed into me. I screamed as my bones shattered and again as my heavy jacket snagged on the grill. My broken sobs continued as the car dragged me down the street.

Why didn't I just go home? I thought as my coat tore, sending me beneath the wheels.

Again the world spun, and my stomach with it, before resolving itself into the familiar sight of stained and cracked plaster clinging to the ceiling above my head.

Home. I was home. In my room, with my back pressed against the locked door. Violent impacts rattled my teeth. I heard the creak of abused wood; one panel splintered. The jagged edge bit into my back before another blow sent me flying across the room.

The door still held, but barely. One more hit and I had no doubt it would give. I sobbed as the metallic tang of blood filled my mouth and shudders rippled through me.

Why had I come home? I had been right to leave the first time, battered but alive. Coming back had not been wise. While I was gone, he had found an aluminum bat somewhere. He had greeted me with it when I had come through the apartment door. Now my right arm hung useless by my side and bright, angry sparks danced before my eyes. New bruises throbbed atop old ones.

Beyond the roaring in my ears I heard my father scream at me through the door.

"You lyin' slut! I know what you been up to, runnin' around all hours of the night. Disappearin' who knows where, just like your godamn mother! I won't have it! Open the door!"

I lunged for the window and eyed the ledge beyond the glass. Right now, three stories up did not seem too high. Not thinking in my fear, I reached for the sash with my broken arm. Agony sliced through me. Sobbing harder, I braced my left hand in the center of the window and heaved. It took two tries and the window squealed in protest.

"What the hell are you doin' in there? You better get your ass over here and open this door!"

The door rattled and groaned as my father applied even more force. With the shriek of splintering wood, it finally gave. I screamed and scrambled out the half-opened window. I had barely enough room to slide through and still crouch on the sill. Desperation weighed in my favor.

Now that he had broken in, only heavy breathing disturbed the silence. My father stalked closer. Panicked, I looked down. The ground seemed much farther away than I had figured. I needed to move to the ledge, but I froze, terrified by the height.

My father took the moment of indecision away from me. His punishing grip locked around my ankle. Bone crushed against bone and I screamed again. My father cursed and shook me. My feet slipped and with it my one-handed grip on the window frame.

I landed hard. Something in my neck snapped right before the molten agony of my shattered back vanished. As my breath bubbled wetly in my ears and my vision fogged over, I thought longingly of the sisters and their parlor. If only I had stayed there instead of going home.

I came to on my hands and knees, a puddle of vomit staining the carpet beneath me an ungodly shade of greenish brown. I pushed myself back and glared at the sisters.

"What did you give me?" I growled through clenched teeth.

The Misses Moirai looked at me with honest sorrow. That unbalanced me further. What was their game?

"We gave you a glimpse." Miss Sis had a gentle rebuke in her tone that even I could not overlook, no matter how rattled I was. She glided past me and took a healthy gulp from my mug. Miss Posie knelt with a rag to clean up the mess I had made while Miss Sis smiled sadly and helped me to my feet.

Her strength astounded me. I stared at all three sisters again and marveled that I had ever thought them old. They had a timelessness about them, but not the weakness of age. I could not remember them being anything other than ancient. They did not appear so now. My confusion grew.

"You best sit, dear."

Miss Clo took my arm. I let her. Once again I found myself ensconced on the divan with the afghan draped around me. I clutched it close. Meeting each of their gazes, I finally spoke. "Why did you show me?"

"You have a third choice," Miss Sis answered.

I remembered what they had said earlier. "But I didn't do either of those things you showed me. Instead I came inside. But you said...you said all my choices lead to death..." I regretted speaking the words.

Miss Sis made a soothing noise, but it was Miss Clo who answered. "This is an interlude, an intervention we are allowed because of who you are...and who you might become. It will lead to a choice, but it is not one in itself."

She spoke in riddles and I found myself more confused. Trying to order my thoughts, I reached for my discarded mug. My extended hand brushed lightly against one of the many pairs of scissors strewn about the room. The fingers tingled again and my eyes went wide with the sensation. That had happened earlier, when I had scratched at the door, and during other visits, as well. What did it mean for me?

"But didn't showing me all this change it?" I asked. "I mean, it isn't like I'd pick either of those choices now, whether I believe those...glimpses, or not."

"This is an interlude. Should you choose to leave, it will be as if none of this took place; you won't remember coming in, you won't remember the glimpses."

"And the third choice you're offering me...doesn't that lead to death, too? You said all my choices lead to death. Why should I choose that one?" I could not keep the hostility out of my tone. "What death would you have me face?"

"Every one from here on out..." Miss Clo answered.

I jerked back. What the hell did that mean?

"And mine would be first."

In shock, my eyes turned toward Miss Posie. Her words were uttered softly, but with longing. She had been silent since the glimpses began. I looked at her more closely; while the other two sisters were fresh and vibrant, there was a haggard edge to Miss Posie's beauty. Her eyes seemed haunted. I had noticed something earlier, but only a hint of it. I found the full force of it heartrending. Miss Posie seemed weary beyond words.

My blood turned to ice and I actually felt myself pale. "What exactly are you asking of me?"

Miss Posie went to her knees before me, earnestness burning in her eyes. "Take my place! Join the Moirai. Free me...."

Free her? Free her?! I scrambled away and felt the bile return to flood the back of my throat. "Ex-cuse me?!"

Again, I nearly leapt up from the couch as next Miss Clo rested her hand upon my shoulder. My gaze darted from sister to sister.

"I think you better explain what's going on now." The sisters caught one another's eye and I felt like an intruder watching them silently decided who would explain.

Finally, Miss Clo spoke, "For Lachesis and myself, the weight of being Fates is slight; we start out knowing the great potential of every mortal, and the many ways they may or may not squander it.

"For dear Atropos, whose task is to sever each mortal coil, being a Fate has become a mighty burden."

"And that's supposed to make me want the job?" I interrupted. "What's that mean, anyway, 'a mighty burden'?"

I cringed as Miss Posie spoke for herself. Her words locked me into her suffering.

"I cannot look upon a face without knowing the choices the person will make. I see the death awaiting them, and why, with no power to change that fate."

The pain in her voice cut to my heart. This was a woman I loved, though clearly I had barely known her. Through that love, her suffering was already my own. But how could I do what they asked of me? How was it even possible?

I was mortal, with a mortal's weaknesses.

"What happens if I say yes?"

"You take up the scissors on the table and snip this thread." Miss Clo answered solemnly as she drew from Miss Posie's finger a delicate ring of braided silk threads that exactly matched the color of the woman's eyes. A part of me marveled that I had never noticed she wore it. I snuck a look at the others' hands and saw empty fingers.

"No one—mortal or divine—can see the rings, unless we take them off."

It unsettled me further to have Miss Sis answer a question I had yet to ask—not that I had intended to. I tried to contain my unease. After all, if what they told me was true, my new knowledge scarcely made me a threat: either this night would change me forever, or I would be dead at the end of it. Hardly the thought to dwell on, but—as mankind was perverse that way—I gave in to the natural impulse.

"And if I say no?"

Though their expressions remained serene, opaque even, the sorrow my question inspired in the three sisters was a tangible thing. Oddly, I sensed that it was as much for my fate as it was for Miss Posie's, whichever option I chose.

"If you say no," Miss Clo answered, "it will be as if you never walked through our door tonight. You will play out the choice you made before I intervened."

I sat in silence as her words sank in. How did they expect me to choose between immediate death and the eternity they offered?

"Why me?" I had not meant to ask, but the question filled the silence until my ears rang with it. My blood pulsed in rhythm. "Why did you pick me for this?"

"Throughout time, I have encountered some few for whom I cannot see the manner of their death," Posie answered in a low, hushed tone, "or at least, I can't until the moment they must choose. You are one of these. That was why I could let myself love you."

My hand drifted above the scissors I had brushed against earlier. I did not touch them, but they became my whole reality while I struggled to choose: to believe? Or not? That was the real challenge here. It would be easier to question my sanity than to buy into their particular madness...if it were not for that annoying tingle. It intensified the closer my hand came to the shears.

Was I strong enough for this? If I picked them up, how long could I resist the despair that had proven too much for this goddess? Then something occurred to me, something very important to my choice.

"Are you them...the three Fates? I mean the first ones? Or has this been done before?"

Miss Sis answered. "We are the true daughters of Zeus and Themis."

My brow drew down into a frown. This had never been done?! Then how did they know it was possible? Or what it would mean for me? Miss Clo interrupted my panicked thoughts.

"Our father has decreed that, should we desire it, and a mortal freely choose to take up our task, that mortal will be as his child and whichever one of us steps down will be free to take her rest."

I thought on what she said. To live forever...to know every person's fate...to be the power destined to remove violent, brutal people from the world. True, not until it was their time, but there was still some satisfaction in that. Too bad it wasn't just the bastards, but everyone...innocents, victims, ordinary people. That would hurt, to sever a worthwhile life, particularly if it were taken by violence. My knowledge of the atrocities mankind was capable of had grown tonight; if I said yes, it would become intimate and without bound.

Then it occurred to me. If these sisters were the Fates, then they knew...

"My mother...." I whispered. I had barely enough air to breath in and out. I clutched the blanket draped around me that much closer. "Where?"

Three sets of eyes flickered to the afghan. What I read in their expressions—anger, sorrow, regret—left me drawing a sharp breath. I did not know if I should cast the blanket from me or refuse to ever let it go. My stomach churned. The sisters did not need to answer aloud. I had not been abandoned then.

"Who?" I spat out, seemingly reduced to speaking only in single words. Again, they did not need to say the words. I ran a chilled hand up and down my right arm, the one my father shattered in the vision.

'Just like your mother!'

Rage echoed in my heart even as my father's words echoed in my mind. My fingers no longer just tingled; they itched to pick up those scissors. What was to stop me from cutting threads who and when I chose? Forget about waiting until his destined time, the bastard would die the moment the scissors were in my hand. What temptation! Think of all the ugliness I could remove from the world!

...Starting with my father. Vengeance urged my hand forward. Conscience tried to pull it back. I was not comfortable with which was stronger. In this moment out of time my own weakness brightly glared. I did not have the purity of intent that the sisters had. They did as they did with innocence and justness. I feared I would not. And what would happen if I were to end up corrupting the natural order of things? A fierce tremor rippled through me. I was honest enough to admit the degree of my own worthiness.

My hand shook violently. With effort, I drew it away and sat back. Through the roaring in my ears I heard a single, weary sigh. Without a word I stood, finding that the rest of me trembled, as well. The sisters rose as one. Miss Clo gathered up her spindle and an afghan I had seen them working on so many times before. Miss Sis searched the table for her tape measure as Miss Posie reached out for the scissors in front of me and slipped them into the pocket of her cardigan. Each of them stepped forward and placed a kiss on my brow, hugged me, and stepped away. Miss Posie waited till last. She offered me a gentle smile and whispered in my ear, "I love you...it's okay, I understand." Then, offered up like a precious gift, she spoke once more. "You were your mother's reason...for saying no."

She brushed her fingertips through my hair and gave me a mini-glimpse of what my fate would have been, had Mum not... disappeared. It was a bittersweet gift and I nearly reached inside

Miss Posie's pocket for the scissors I had moments ago refused to take up. She gripped my hand before I could, giving it a gentle, knowing squeeze.

A single, wrenching sob escaped me and I clung to her the longest of the three. If I did not already know my fate, it would have killed me to know I had let Miss Posie down. But she had had a hand in raising me, to some extent, along with her sisters. She had helped to instill in me the strength to turn my back on my own weakness.

"I love you, too," I managed to choke out. "I am so sorry it cannot be me."

Miss Posie lowered her forehead to rest against mine and I drank in the comfort of her acceptance. Neither of us uttered another word. When it was time she squeezed my hand in farewell and followed her sisters out of the room.

Finally, I stood alone in the parlor. I said goodbye to my haven of comfort. I took a final sip of cocoa. I buried my nose one last time in the blanket and said a long overdue farewell to Mum, before letting myself out.

Stronger than I had been when I had arrived this night, I walked into the darkness to embrace my fate.

LUNA

Pale white sister
Against a faded blue sky
Resignedly watching
As your golden brother
Steals your glory
You quietly back away
From his gaudy, glaring brilliance
Timid in your own perfection

RUBY RED

THERE WAS BLOOD ON THE COUNTER. JUST THREE LITTLE DROPS, bright and deep all at once. Startling against the white marble. I ran my finger through one gleaming half-globe. It smeared a red spectrum along the edge of the sink.

I giggled. The sound startled me. It was out of place in the surrounding starkness, slashing a hole in the silence that closed in an instant. I was being disrespectful. Dragging my lower lip between my teeth I reached for the roll of tissue and tore off a couple of squares. With great care I wiped away the smear I'd made, leaving the remaining two drops pristine and the rest of the counter nothing but white. I balled the tissue and clutched it tight in my fist.

The urge to giggle swept through me once more and I ground down harder on my lip. The pain was sharp and focusing. It allowed me to fight back the urge. It had been so long since I'd been allowed color. They didn't trust me with color. Things happened.

I wrapped my arms tight around my body and stared at the remaining two drops. Lost myself in the play of light upon the gleaming surfaces. They sparkled like gems. My breath quickened and I had to tuck my hands beneath my arms to keep them still, to keep them from reaching out and playing with the pretty color.

"Red," I whispered. It was no more than a breath, nearly just a thought. I didn't want anyone to hear. They would take the drops away. "Red...red like rubies, like poppies under the sun, strawberries dripping with dew."

The intensity ran like a wire up my spine. Each word drew it taut; each image sprang into my mind and spawned more. I buried my senses in each thing that surfaced. My eyes were dazzled by the glimmer of jewels, my nose filled with the smell of warm flowers, my tongue savored the sweetness of ripe fruit.

"Red!"

The bathroom became a sea of red as my mental images shaped reality. Flower petals scattered over the cold, white tile; ripe fruit crushed beneath my feet as I circled the room. Power swirled around me, brushed my skin, danced among the strands of my hair. It was red as well. Everything was red.

I laughed with the joy of color. The white was swept away. Bending, I scooped my hands through the redness and encountered sharp-edge gems. I'd found my rubies. The sting of pain was life and I laughed more. Gone was the sterile white. I lifted my arms, pale, white skin trailing beads of blood from a hundred little nicks.

"Red! Red like blood!"

The bite of iron overwhelmed my other senses. The smell, the taste, the slick, thick feel of it against my skin. A liquid red tide swept over me, coating the walls and sweeping away fruit and flowers and gems.

"Red...red like blood," I whispered again, a mere moving of the lips, drowned out by the pulse of the tide.

Red swept me away.

PORTRAIT OF
A GREEN MOTHER

A ravaged beauty
cloaked in a patchwork mockery
of her former splendor
a crown of timeless flowers
woven in what is left of her hair
with one hand she cradles humanity
the other fends off society's blows

On "Purgatory"

This story is one of my favorites. I can't tell you why. Well, I could, actually, but I shouldn't. I'll explain. I hate spoilers. As I reread the following tale to prepare to write this piece, I found myself constantly editing before I even began ... you can't mention that, that gives too much away, you shouldn't—no, not that! I can't say an actual word about what goes on in this story without in some way ruining, at least a little, the experience to follow. Please, just trust me, there are some stories that, even knowing the location in which they're set before you begin reading is too much.

This is one to be read like we used to in the old days, for the sheer, breathless thrill of reading. No series, no need for knowing the genre, no need for anything but eyes and the time to waste on the frivolous pursuit of enjoyment. Ah... I remember those bygone days well. Like I remember this story.

It is one of the finest, self-contained set-pieces ever written. Instantly intriguing, fast-paced, noble—honest. They don't come any better. Enjoy.

—C.J. Henderson,
author of the
Teddy London, Jack Hagee,
and *Piers Knight* series

PURGATORY

Purgatory is when
something inside of you
is certain you've been damned.
Hell is when it's right.

HEAT...SUFFOCATING HEAT... I CANNOT BREATHE. MY CHEST heaves and my hands claw frantically. I am burning up and I cannot fight free. Visions of fire crowd my panic-stricken mind. Vibrant flames paint the darkness behind my eyes while the stench of burning human hair weaves past my nostrils. I feel the whimper before I hear the muffled scream. It takes a moment to realize both come from me.

Harsher shrieks of laughter slam into me and disperse the panic that keeps me trapped in my nightmare. I know that chorus...intimately. Rage displaces my fear. I buck and thrash. My clawing hands curl into equally impotent fists.

The blankets swaddle me, trapping my hands by my side. What little breath I have is forced from my chest. My mouth gaps, but draw in only foul cotton, rather than dank air. I go still and taut. Struggling only binds me tighter. Atop the thin cover, a weight pins me to the bed; that weight, in turn, holds a pillow across my face. I twist in my involuntary cocoon, my body in one direction and my face the other. I manage an insufficient breath. One final, massive heave and I dump the night hag to the floor. The blanket tears from where she has tucked it beneath the cot. The already-frayed edges shred as I scramble from the tangle and plant my back against the corner wall. The chill creeps through my thin shirt and into my bones. Will alone suppresses the shivers traveling up my spine.

Malice hisses from the narrow strip of floor. I hear the scrape of claws upon concrete as the hag rights herself. I brace for attack, my muscles taut and ready, my chin lowering.

My vision adjusts to the meager light from the corridor outside my cell. At least enough to see the form crouched on the floor, faintly striped by bars of low light and shadow. The binding runes scribed about her neck—the ones that bind her to her cell—have been blurred, the surrounding flesh blistered. Someone has given the hag a brief reprieve, allowing her out to play. For a while, anyway.... The lines of the symbols are starting to sharpen once more. Soon the compulsion written into her flesh will repair itself and force her to return to her confinement.

My attention goes back to the familiar features of the one on the floor. One catlike eye stares out from a lined face just above a jaw outthrust and vaguely leonine; the other eye is lost in a marbling of scar tissue that obscures half the hag's face and leaves wide furrows to wrap around her head and through her straggly yellow hair.

I snarl and visualize my fingers making those wounds bleed again. I can see in my mind's eye, my nails leaving fresh marks across that hideous face. My anger demands her other eye. But that is wrong; my anger does not rule me.

"This treachery gains you nothing, Kala," I growl, keeping my voice low, as not to draw the attention of the guards. "You'll still be dogsbody to all the others."

Kala hisses at the double insult.

This is a test. I am new on the Block and my rebellion is a constant challenge. I am not as ruthless, as vicious as the others, just stronger. Smarter. And luckier, perhaps. Definitely more determined. So far, I refuse to be buried beneath the coils of the prison hierarchy. I do not challenge, but neither do I bow down. No one much likes that. Too bad.

A sound from the corridor ends the stalemate. The thud of heavy footsteps on concrete draws closer. The hag shrinks in upon herself. She becomes more catlike in size and posture and slides out between the bars of my cell. The guard stomps by just moments later, intent on something other than me. He doesn't yell, so he hadn't noticed Kala either.

Where is he headed then? What mischief is about? Had Kala been meant to make me a diversion? If so, whoever had helped her blur the runes will be furious. I unfold myself from the corner and creep nearer the bars. More guards hurry past in the direction of the first. The phantom scent of singed hair grows stronger. Not a part of the nightmare, then. In a cell nearby someone has burned. My hands clench and I swallow hard. I press close to the bars in an effort to see what I can of the Block.

Most of it is beyond my view. The cells I can see are steeped in darkness, the corridors hardly brighter. I catch furtive shifting in the shadows and know no one sleeps. They wait and watch. I catch the barest hint of an orange flicker reflecting off the grey cinder-block walls to my left. The smell of burning flesh intensifies.

Two cells down there is a whoosh, followed by a roar. The sullen, smoldering glow flares with an infernal intensity. I flinch away and release the bars of my cell, half expecting them to burn me. I hear the laughter of the guards and fall back further into the shadow.

"Another flamer! It's almost getting boring."

"Oh, right," one gravelly voice grumbles. "That's why you're the first to claim your slot in the Pool, yeah?"

"You're just chapped because he always takes the one you have your eye on," another guard laughs, "and mostly wins."

"But what I want to know," the first guard says, ignoring the jab. "Is what happened to the variety?"

"What do you expect? Once they give up hope, it's over. And they all pretty much believe in the same version these days, however much they believe at all...."

"Enough, already."

Hearing this last voice, I slip back under the thin covers and turn toward the wall. The voice belongs to Cerb, the guard in charge of the night shift. I lay there in the dark and strain my ears, hoping to hear the voices recede down the corridor. Instead, the footsteps stop outside my cell. I grit my teeth and fight for stillness, for the illusion of sleep. It is no good.

"Rouse a clean-up crew, starting with this one, seeing as she's awake," Cerb orders before she disappears down the corridor.

I flinch.

My cell opens with the grate of metal on stone. I roll to a sitting position as the bars clang against the end of their track. Before the guards can enter the cell to 'rouse' me, I am at the entrance waiting for instruction, my face impassive. I know better than to give them cause to dispense worse treatment than they will already. The guards are massive, three times the breadth and height of a mortal man, though only twice the size of me. Even so, I keep my gaze averted, vague. I reserve my defiance for my fellow damned and leave the devils alone.

As I stand there, the guard closest to me reaches out an enormous, thick-skinned hand. His flesh is the charcoal color that falls between a normal grey and true black. An obsidian claw tips each finger. All but one curls under; the one extended bites into the flesh at my neck and carves a caveat into my binding runes. The wound burns as if the claw tip is salt-coated. My pained hiss brings satisfied grins to the guards' faces. I fight to keep my lip from lifting in an answering snarl. Instead, I look down at the trickle of deep crimson drawn from my bruise-black skin and mentally dub this guard Char-claw. After all, names have power, even those given by another.

"Follow me," Char-claw rumbles. His gaze is flat and hard. Clearly, he hopes I will not comply. I am not stupid, or suicidal, for that matter. I follow him to the cell two down from my own. The other guards break away, each heading for separate cells. A shifting in the shadows tells me those are occupied. The one in front of me is void of movement. No, not empty, though. Past the bars I see the sullen glow of embers in the process of dying. I swallow hard. Char-claw mutters something and a dull light fills the cell. The bars rattle open, but I go no closer, nor will I, until I am ordered.

Before the other guards return with the rest of the detail, I force myself to stare at the ashen outline of a body delineated on the unmarred cot. The term 'blast-shadow' comes to mind...only this has substance. I clamp down on the urge to retch. I can already feel the fine, clinging motes coating my skin. My throat clogs with the ash that has yet to fill the air. I grit my teeth and force the phantom sensations away. I must impose control before I begin to feel my flesh crisp and end up screaming my weakness to my adversaries.

The clang of cells opening sounds behind me. A sharp-drawn breath follows shortly, chased by the guards' mocking laughter. Someone has not borne the marking well.

I feel the hard, discouraging expression I have cultivated around the other inmates automatically settle into place as they approach. My transformation does not go unnoticed. Several feet away, Char-claw smirks and flexes the finger with which he had marked me. Fresh agony spears from the gash. I set my teeth against making a sound, then hold my breath and wait out the pain.

He seems mildly amused at the neutral gaze I turn to him. There is a taut moment between us. Then one of my fellow inmates mutters petulantly from inside the cell. "All of us...for this?"

It is Kala.

Kala is an idiot.

Char-claw looks away from me. The pain from my wound instantly fades to a dull ache, but I do not relax. My eyes remain trained upon the guard and his expression. Yes. Kala is definitely an idiot.

He takes one step forward. The hag instinctively cringes down, cowering by the cot. Char-claw sneers and his long arm snaps forward and angles up. The talons rake Kala across her withered chest. Blood sprays the walls of the cell and flicks upon all of us outside, a warm, salty sprinkle that burns like acid. Kala shrieks and crumbles to the floor, whimpering at the further ruin of her body, trembling in shock. I wait for the light to die in her eyes, but they continue to smolder as blood pools about her on the floor.

The guard's hand lashes out again and Kala's hatred flees, replaced by terror. She collapses upon herself, a small, shaking mound huddling on the floor. A high-pitched keen fills the cell. Char-claw laughs as he snags the sheet from the cot, sending the ashes billowing into the air.

"That should be enough to keep all of you occupied," he sneers as he thrusts the sheet toward the inmate behind me. "Bind her wound up with that and get her to work.

"You!" he snaps in my direction. "Fetch the cleaning supplies."

I gladly back away, turning at the last minute, waiting to feel his claws score my own flesh once more. The blow does not come. My head jerks back as if it had, though, upon seeing who else makes up the detail. I do not recognize the slight figure tucked back among the shadows, but the other, her I know all too well. The guards have roused Deth, the self-proclaimed ruler of the Block. Her fists clench on the sheet Char-claw had thrust at her. Her small, poison-yellow eyes snap from Kala to me as I head for the closet at the end of the corridor where the mops and rags and cleaners are locked away. I can feel her displeasure twine around my limbs, dragging down upon me in a constant effort to subdue, to make me subservient. I flex those muscles and release my grip on the rage flowing through me. The threads of her will burn away and I hear her furious hiss. I do not look back.

I start down the corridor, one of the other guards shadowing me, treading close enough to catch my heels at every step. This one is Char-claw's double in all but the color of his skin, which is purplish red, like a blood-engorged cock. That—and his attitude—earns him the name The Dick. His breath is hot and heavy on my neck. I clench my teeth and force myself not to whirl on him like a cornered wolverine. I stop facing the closet, just to the side so he can unlock it.

My "shadow" continues forward until I find myself pinned to the wall. I buck and snarl the instant I feel trapped. His hand snakes around to crush my breast in a brutal grope and he moans into my ear, "Oh yeah, that's right...I love it that you fight." Then The Dick earns his name even more as he laughs and presses his groin tight against my ass. Only threadbare fabric shields me.

I go still, but for a faint trembling I cannot control. My jaw clenches tight against many curses as I struggle to distance myself inside, because there is no hope of doing so physically.

The guard laughs again. His tongue flicking out and across my cheek. Thick and sinuous, it strafes my flesh until it stings.

"You had a little something there…a bit sour, but then, it wasn't yours, was it? A pity, that." I jerk in disgust as I realize he has licked Kala's spattered blood from my skin.

His tongue slides over me again and dips into my ear suggestively. I cannot hold back my shudder. He moans in appreciation and grinds his crotch against me harder, as if he would impale me through our clothes. He reaches around with his other hand to grab me harshly between my thighs.

Even the trembling stops. I go tense and wooden, waiting for the pain.

"Hey!" Char-claw calls from down the corridor. "She's out to clean up, not play. This is already going to take too long, thanks to this one here." There is a thump, and Kala moans. "You want to be the one to explain to Cerb why this is taking all night?"

"Aw, man…come on, this one fights it so good! Just a little…you can even watch."

I force myself not to fight him. It will only goad him on, encourage him to disregard Char-claw's order. The other guard is silent. All I can hear is the heavy panting of The Dick behind me and Kala's continuing whimper. How ironic that earlier she'd tried to kill me only to be my possible salvation now. I hold myself so rigid I feel like stone, no movement but my steady, controlled breaths as I wait for Char-claw's judgment.

"Don't care what you do after orders are carried out, but for now quit screwing around."

The Dick lets out a deep chuckle and grinds himself harder against me, grinding until even my bones threatened to give beneath his thrust. "Soon, then, soon I'll do that lovely ass right." His hand sweeps up away from my breast to brush across my cheek in a deceptively gentle caress that ends in a flick from his razor-edged claw. My head rings with his moan as his tongue flickers out to catch the trail of fresh blood. I swallow hard, fighting revulsion and rage in equal measure.

"Mmmm…" he murmurs once more for my ear alone. "Now that is sweet. Can't wait to try out the rest."

My breath comes fast and shallow. I shudder ever so slightly. It has nothing to do with fear; I struggle not to lash out. The Dick finally unlocks the closet and I gather the necessary supplies, my expression blank and my eyes lowered.

The other guards and inmates watch as the two of us make our way back to the cell. The odor of blood and ash assails me from two cells down. I close my mind to the stench and tell myself no dust clogs my throat. Deth grabs for the thick-handled broom the moment I draw close. I tighten my grip on the mop and thrust the bucket and rags to the unfamiliar inmate, ignoring Kala, who is useless even without injuries.

"Here, we'll need water."

The other inmate looks at me with a gaze as dark and deep as forever, but does not take the supplies I hold out to her. Her expression bears no malice, no defiance I can see, only surprise. I give her the eye. Where does she come from? I know every inmate here like I know my own face. She is a stranger, un-familiar. Her pale skin seems to glow like something pure and good against the backdrop of the hellhole surrounding us. She seems distinctly out of place. Of course, I have learned that a pleasant package on the outside is just as likely to hide a rotten core. Hard to say if that is the case here. There is something else off about her though that I cannot pinpoint. I try, but she speaks and her words distract me. They sound far-off, as if she is not even here.

"Hasn't this gone long enough?"

My lip curls. As innocent as she sounds, apparently this pale, insubstantial wraith thinks she is going to mess with me and I will just take it. She reminds me of my brother, Payne. The features are different, obviously, but the attitude is the same. Of course, my brother is dead...because of me. Because I failed to protect him...because I'd been angry over one of his mind games. I'd had to watch as he burned.

I do not like the reminder.

"Just take the friggin' bucket and fill it with water." I snarl. "They tagged you for this detail, and you'll pull your weight like the rest of us."

She ignores my words. "Aren't you ready to come home?"

"Oh, yeah, right!" I spit at her, rattling the bucket with a hard shake. "What are you, my conscience? Water! Now!"

Behind me, I hear Deth laugh, followed by two warm, wet streams drenching the back of my hand and pelting the wooden sides of the bucket. I give the Wraith a black look as the bottom of the container fills with rancid piss.

Char-claw and The Dick burst out laughing as they shake the final drops off their cocks and slip them back into their pants. "Now fill it up right before we finish filling it for you."

I shoot a brutal look toward the Wraith, silently promising retribution, as I never have before. I am shoved from behind hard enough to slop the contents of the bucket down my legs. It is getting harder to keep silent. And harder still not to whirl upon my persecutors.

"Now!" Char-claw roars. "Before I change my mind about letting my buddy here play first."

I move in tight, angry steps toward the crude basin set in the cell wall. It serves double-duty as both sink and squatter. I lean the mop against the wall and dump the piss down the bowl, sloshing in some soap, then refilling the bucket with hard, rusty water. The soap fizzes, leaving a thin, skuzzy film across the surface. Like this shithole will ever be clean anyway. We are on this detail just to add to the hell of our existence.

I turn and Deth is behind me, mucking up my mop, swirling it in the splotches of blood and ash. The patterns that form are disturbing, but not as disturbing as the look on her face. Talk about malice. She strokes the handle of the mop suggestively and looks me up and down. Her lip curls in a sneer and her tongue flicks along the edge of her teeth.

"You think you're better than all of us, don't you? Don't you believe it, slut," Deth hisses, her mottled skin rippling as she gets up in my face. "You'll lift your ass for him; just like the rest, you'll take it. And whether you fight or not, you're giving him what he wants.

"He's gonna teach you your place, and when he's done, I'm gonna remind you what it is every chance I get." She strokes the handle once more, ending the motion a foot down the length. The look in her eyes goes bright and lethal as she flexes her power- ful wrist. The wood snaps and she slides the short piece into her pants, never taking her eyes off mine. She pats where it lays along her inner thigh, and then reaches out as if to stroke my cheek.

I jerk back with a snarl. Deth just laughs and rubs the bulge again. "This here's for you...you think about that, think about it a lot, sweetheart. You weren't smart enough to drop dead, so now you're gonna be my bitch, after he's had his fun."

She lets go of the mop, which falls against my chest. Reflexively, I grab it, before the guards notice, covering the splintered end with my fist. Deth laughs again and takes up her unblemished broom, turning her back on me as if I am no threat. I struggle not to leap forward and show her how wrong she is. My hand crushes the remaining mop handle until the sound of grinding wood fills the cell.

Five minutes...five minutes alone together and Deth will never again haunt me. I fight the urge. My gaze drifts across the blood spatters and ash. It travels fleetingly over the guards, bullshitting outside the cell. I will not bring myself down to this. I refuse to let them twist me into something vicious and brutal. A few deep breaths and the application of much will power disperses the tide of fury threatening to overwhelm me.

The Dick never does get to...play.

By the time we mop up the blood and ash, restoring the cell to its former lackluster state, Cerb returns.

"What's taking so long?" she rumbles.

I stand silently to the back. My hand hides the damaged mop handle from her view. I watch without staring as her dark ebony eyes scan the restored, uniform grey of worn stone, dingy mattress, and iron bars. Her hard gaze sharpens as it draws down once more on where we stand, coming to rest upon Char-claw. I try to read the expression in her flat, muscular face, looking for a clue in the widening jaw that gives this guard the unreadable look of a pit bull. All I can be sure of is I do not want her attention focused on me. I get the impression from the tick in Char-claw's jaw that he shares my sentiment.

"The crew took some persuading."

"Well, they've persuaded themselves out of their morning meal; breakfast hour is over. Get them down to the Yard."

Silently, I gather the cleaning supplies, hiding the broken handle behind the bristles of the up-turned broom. With my arms unavoidably laden, I fall in behind the guards as they lead us from the cell. Deth follows close behind me. It takes an effort to not clench my jaw as my neck bristles in reaction to the enemy at my back. I slow as we near the supply closet, waiting for The Dick to open it once more. My nemesis closes the distance. She comes to a halt right behind me, with not a breath of space between us. The hard bulge of the broken-off handle nestles along my ass. She starts to roll her hips in clear mimicry of The Dick's earlier assault. With a fierce scream I arch away from her and spin around, my fist slamming into her jaw before I can even think. The first crunch is satisfying.

The second: agony.

I roll my head back carefully and look up from the crumpled mound I have become on the corridor floor. The blow had hit hard and fast out of nowhere. I turn empty eyes toward Deth, skimming over her like she is nothing, and settle my gaze on Cerb's cudgel. So, that is what hurt like a motherfucker.

"Seems you make a habit of defacing prison property." Her tone is cold and intractable. Her eyes glide to the side. I look in the same direction and see the mop, fully visible at Deth's feet, and shake my head, more to clear it, than in denial.

Whack! Another smack from the cudgel and my jaw becomes a conduit for the electric fire shooting down my spine. A hand locks on my collar and yanks my head up until I stare Deth in the face. Her expression is filled with contrived pain, its falseness betrayed by the glimmer of satisfaction lurking in the far depths of her eyes.

"Every inmate in this place is prison property," Cerb rumbles low and menacing, like the precursor to a landslide. "You do not damage the goods, understood?"

My gaze flickers from the thin tendril of blood snaking down Deth's jaw to the blood-soaked sheet wrapping Kala's chest. I can feel more than a trickle trailing down my neck. Apparently the guards can break their own toys, but heaven help anyone else that even scuffs them. I clench my jaw and fight down my fury, internalizing the infernal burn. Letting it show would be like placing a weapon in Deth's hand or begging Cerb to strike me down again. Neither bitch needs any help from me.

"Understood?" The cudgel unsubtly rose.

"Yes."

"Put this shit away and get down to the Yard," Cerb orders as she nudges the fallen supplies. Her eyes linger a moment on the ragged end of the mop handle, but she says nothing more.

The Yard.

I hate it.

The Yard is where Deth and her rivals hold Court. Deth rules her Block ruthlessly and against any opposition, as did the others. They have to or they will be pulled down. That's why I piss Deth off. I never really challenge her; I merely decline to play prison politics. For that very reason I stand in the way of her supreme rule.

Tough shit.

As I enter the Yard two things catch my eye: Deth holding Court over by the far wall, and the Wraith lurking by the prison door, closely watching everything going on. What I am about to do breaks a taboo, but I do not much care to be polite at the moment. I stalk over to the Wraith and bring my face down to hers. "Welcome to Hell...what did you do to end up here?"

"This isn't Hell," she answers softly, ignoring my antagonism. "It's Purgatory. Don't let them tell you any different because you aren't damned...yet, you just think you are." The look she gives me is intent. Her eyes shimmer with purity and compassion—neither of which I buy—and her lips draw down ever so slightly in a frown. "You balance on the edge. That's why they push you so hard."

A harsh bark of laughter slips past my lips. "Well isn't that a nice and delusional analogy, next thing you know, you'll be telling me everything is really sunshine and posies and this is a bad dream." With a sneer tugging at my mouth, I turn my back on her and make my way to the far corner, away from Deth and away from the Wraith and as alone as I can be in a crowded prison yard.

I wipe my face of expression and settle back to watch the show. No doubt there will be one, there always is of some sort or another. Posturing and power plays abound. I might not participate, but I would be a fool to ignore the subtle shifts going on around me.

The crowd around Deth is thick this day. They hover like crows outside a slaughterhouse. Some shift closer, craning their necks in rapt and eager fascination. Others stand taut and still, their eyes darting uneasily away and back again, as if they watch in spite of themselves. The murmurs of the crowd reach me clear across the courtyard. The sound of something hard repeatedly slamming something soft follows, entwining with pained gasps that fall away to whimpers.

My head goes up and my shoulders tense. With each hit the wounds gained by Cerb's hand throb in sympathy. My flaring nostrils draw the tang of copper from the air until I taste it on my tongue. I cannot see it for fmyself, but blood is being drawn, spattering in the dust of the Yard. Clotting the air. Shrieks rise high. Familiar shrieks.

Kala...paying for her failure. Paying for her stupidity with the guards. Paying for each breath I continue to draw and the rape I have so far escaped.

My jaw grinds with a sound like rock crushing rock. Tension sings through my limbs and I find myself stepping away from the wall. Kala suffers because of me. She might very well die in the dust surrounded by the ghouls watching on. I have been here before, faced with this conflict. I take a step forward as guilt again twists my gut.

No! She tried to kill me last night; she will try again if she survives Deth's beating. So what if she has, for now, saved me from The Dick; that was through her own stupidity, rather than any purposeful effort on her part. I force myself to relax, to remain where I am.

I owe Kala nothing.

I tell myself that over and over, yet what I hear are the Wraith's words drifting through my thoughts like mist rising from the moist ground: You aren't damned...yet. Not yet. I try to remind myself she is delusional. Like I have any reason to believe her. Knowing my own sins, belief is nearly impossible. But believe her or not, and no matter my offenses in the past, I am not like the others: I defend myself against the bullies...I do not strike down those who are weaker.

Nor do I have it in me to stand by while others do so.

My determined stride carries me forward. I have pretended it is not so, but all along I have let Deth rule my actions, just like she does all the others. With a menacing growl rumbling in my throat, I push my way through the crowd. I am hardly aware as they close ranks behind me. The scene at the center of the makeshift arena holds all of my attention. Deth stands with legs wide spread and arm raised, the length of mop handle fisted in her hand, ready to backhand Kala.

I cannot suppress my gasp. My body clenches, taut with tension. Kala lays like a puddle on the ground, more pulp than person. Only the sound of her whistling breath betrays the fact that she is still alive.

Great. Another one who reminds me of Payne.

"Enough!" Guilt and anger crackle in my voice.

Deth lowers her improvised cudgel. The crowd falls silent.

"Looks like I'm the one who gets the pleasure of teaching you your place, after all." She slides toward me and strikes lightning-fast. I block the blow with one arm and slam my other fist into her jaw.

Our audience gasps and I allow contempt to flow across my expression. "You teach me what not to be, nothing more."

I move across the clearing, placing myself between her and Kala. Inmates from all over the Yard start drifting closer to join those from our Block. The leaders push to the fore, with those they rule gathering behind.

Tension crackles through the crowd as everyone waits for the balance of power to shift. I know better. The power does not shift...the focus does. Some of Deth's people creep forward and I tense. I can take a few of them at once, but not the entire Block.

Those that rule the other Blocks clear their throats and move as one to intervene. I have not been there long, but certainly long enough to know they view this as a challenge and if Deth cannot hold her power against me alone, the others will not allow her to hold it with the help of her "subjects".

I curse Kala silently. I want no part of the power plays that drive prison society, but now I have no choice. I should have ignored Deth's punishment circle, but no matter how treacherous Kala is, she does not deserve such brutality.

Deth, obviously, disagrees.

My adversary launches herself across the distance separating us. The rounded end of the stick slams into my gut before I can move. I ignore the pain and grab Deth's wrist, twisting it hard.

She shrieks. Her eyes glow with hatred as she strikes at me with her other fist. I laugh and shove her away. She rages and the crowd shifts. Deth spits at me. Where she strikes bare skin, my arm burns. The muscles beneath tingle until all sensation deadens. I curse and scrub the spot against the tail of my shirt. She makes to spit again and I backhand her. An angry hiss splits the air and Deth launches a physical attack engaging everything from fists and improvised cudgel to her powerful legs. I evade what I can and bear the blows that strike with an empty expression, giving her nothing. She makes to pummel my face with the wooden cudgel. I pull back only to gasp with shock: a ribbon of agony slices down my cheek. Burning drops fall from my jaw and the smell of fresh blood floods my senses. I roar and lunge at her. Sheer mass on my side, I bear her to the ground. My fists slam into her repeatedly before I tear the mop handle from her grasp. The other end has been worked to a vicious point. I growl and my grip flexes on the length of wood.

My nerves are taut and my ears catch sounds of movement around me. Pinning Deth to the ground with one massive hand wrapped around her throat and the weight of my body crushed against her torso, I turn my head to gauge the secondary threat.

Our clearing has grown smaller.

I give the crowd a quelling look. Let them see the menace swirling beneath my skin. A wave of unease sweeps through them. I take in the nervous shifting, stare down a few baleful glares. I turn my gaze back toward Deth. "Kala is off limits; you've punished her enough."

Deth chuckles low and evil. Triumph lights her eyes and her thin, hard lips tweak in a dismissive smirk. "You think so, do you?"

Behind me a sick, muffled thud sounds. It is followed by a crunch, and by cruel laughter. I twist around, my hand tightening reflexively upon Deth's throat. Her henchmen have crept in to carry out her bidding while my attention has been on their leader. My eyes lock on Kala's slack face, her lifeless eye. Blood trails down her chin from the corner of her mouth. Payne's face superimposes itself over the macabre sight, like a phantom floating in my mind's eye, damning me. I scream and gnash my teeth. Rage trembles through my limbs and hope flees before it. I am finally damned in truth. I have failed once more to protect. It has never been my strong suite.

But vengeance...I am real good at vengeance.

I loosen my grip on the makeshift cudgel until the blunt end is in my palm and the sharpened end is clear. Intent fills my eyes: anger, rage, vengeance, malice...I allow all of that to flow through me until my raised arm vibrates with their dark power.

Down it plunges, buried all the way to the blunt end in my nemesis's chest. Blood pools around my fingers, searing them. The tingling burn travels up my arm and straight to my heart, where all sensation dies.

I stand. Taking up my new mantle, I turn damned eyes upon my new subjects.

"I am Deth...bow down before me."

DEATH

Death trails behind me
in a slow, stately march
unconcerned I'll draw away
beyond his reach
he is the spider in the web
some he takes swiftly
while others linger
escape is an illusion
a hopeful lie
I whisper to myself

On "Stoli and Solitude"

Ever wonder how you would get by without the one who often saves you from yourself? Within Stoli and Solitude we find more than just a man suffering from regret and remorse. In a few thousand words, Danielle explores the loss of love, the value of a stiff drink, and how we remember the ghosts of our past. We also learn that sometimes the biggest hearts come in the smallest of packages.

—Tonia Brown,
author of the *Railroad!* Serial

STOLI AND SOLITUDE

Fredrich was puzzled. It had been on the table…of that he was certain. He could picture it even now, virgin and pure and ready. Now it was gone. He could see the ring…the thin little ring of darkened maple where even the air cried as it tried to grasp the smooth glass, only to find itself sliding, soaking into old, dry wood.

Matilda would have scolded. She would have batted him with her dishrag and thrust his glass into his hand so she could wipe the table—after claiming half his drink. He missed Matilda. Holy Lord, did he miss Matilda. He knew how much she'd loathed the taste of vodka, yet she always drank half that he would not suffer from the whole. He only had so much. Strictly rationed. He never poured more than one glass a night. Had never poured more than one glass a night…

Much had changed without his Matilda there to save him from himself.

Puzzled, bleary eyed, Fredrich searched the room from where he perched. The dusty armchair was something else Matilda would have scolded him for. 'Such a thing! You bring such a thing into my nice, clean house? What would you do with it? It is not fit even for dogs!" Her dark brown eyes would have laughed and danced as she said it. Then she would have taken out her broom and whacked at the chair until not a puff of dust was left to escape into the air. Silent tears ran down his face. He would gladly give up the chair, if only Matilda were there to frown upon it.

Where was his tumbler? It had taken such effort to get up to pour it to begin with. Must he do it again? Long gone were the days of only one glass a night. And this time he had not even gotten to drink the first one. Down came his hand upon the worn arm; up puffed a cloud of dust.

A little sneeze filled the endless silence of his solitary room. Fredrich blinked, braced his hands on the arms of his chair, and leaned forward, his expression even more confused. Another sneeze, as the dust continued to settle. Pushing to his feet with much effort, he crossed himself and turned slowly around and around.

Perhaps it was not too much effort to pour another glass. Yes...he would have another glass, this time to drink.

With slow, old-man steps, the young man started forward, only to stop in stunned amazement. What he had not seen before were the faint lines of moisture marking his table. Not the ring...that he saw clearly where his glass should have been. These lines disappeared behind Matilda's picture, lines drawn in the dust by a trailing edge of condensation not given the time to pool.

As Fredrich peered harder, his Dido's tales of fairies and bobkins unfurled in his memory, throwing up as much dust as the armchair. The sight he saw was peculiar: a tiny brown mouse straining against the side of his tumbler, pushing and pushing until its little heart could be seen slamming against its ribs, and still it pushed. And Fredrich watched, bemused. Watched as the crash of delicate crystal spattered the floor. He jerked back and nearly fell.

He too would have shattered. Only hadn't he already? Sweet Jesus, Matilda. Sweet Jesus, did he miss her.

The brown mouse turned, breathing heavy, like a bull. Astounding for something so small. Its large round eyes were like warm chocolate...dark and wet and hot. There was anger and hurt in those eyes. And still Fredrich didn't understand. Feeling he needed it...deserved it even more, he reached for another heirloom tumbler and set it upon the table. Next his hand went to the bottle of Stoli.

Before he could pour the first ounce, that peculiar mouse thrusted for all it was worth against the second glass, moving it from beneath the flow of precious, costly vodka, Fredrich tried again, just shifting the bottle. The mouse shoved harder.

It was so surreal that, even knowing how it would end, Fredrich kept following the glass, until it too tumbled to the floor. All those shards...all that wasted vodka...and all Fredrich could think was: 'I recognize those eyes.'

He placed the bottle on the table for the last time. With one hand he tightened the cap. With the other he reached down, then held his breath.

Exhausted, Matilda crept into his hand and laid her tear-slick cheek against his thumb.

On "Emberling"

Never beg to know a secret if you aren't prepared to hear the answer. In *Emberling*, Danielle Ackley-McPhail weaves a magical world of loss and magic. An orphaned child yearns to know who her parents really were and why they died. Seeking the answer takes her into dangerous territory, and uncovers a secret that will change her life forever. A poignant fantasy tale in a mystical world that will leave you wanting more.

—Gail Z. Martin,
author of *Reign of Ash*,
co-author of *Iron and Blood*

EMBERLING

They Fled Draigbyr in the early hours before dawn, when the ember oaks still glowed the faint red of banked coals where the sap ran close to the surface. Sleepy and confused, eight-year-old Camirel clutched the pouch newly hung about her neck as she followed Popi and Mam through the forest. All around them a pack of embrils, the giant dragon-like lizards that shared their valley, kept pace with them, huffing and growling in agitation, their heads swinging back and forth as if they looked for a foe to fight.

The embrils did not like people but Popi and Mam had always told her they didn't count as normal people. They were Celdraig, an ancient order of runecasters who kept the lore of dragons. Mam said at one time their kind had served the dragons, cared for them, but not anymore.

No dragon had been seen for many generations before Cami's birth.

But they were still Celdraig, anyway, which meant they were dragon people and the embrils liked them.

"I don't want to go to Mabet," Cami muttered. Her voice trembled and she fought against the frown tugging at her face. She was frightened and she did not understand. She stopped at one clearing and stared up at her parents. "Please, I don't want to leave." Tears brimmed in eyes the color of coal ash but did not fall. She could not keep her lip from quivering.

Popi stopped, but did not turn. Instead he stood with his legs braced and a thicket scythe clutched in both hands as if he were ready to clear saplings. His shoulders shook. Mam spun around and knelt before Cami, face pale and strained and her eyes bright, but dry. "You must, my little emberling...you must. Now hurry, Brother Rolfo is waiting."

"But why?"

Mam worried her lip and her gaze darted among the trees and back. "Camirel, I need you to trust me, I need you to go for a while so I'll know you're safe."

Cami lost her battle with the frown. "I'm safe here. The dragon keeps us safe."

Her father tensed but did not turn.

"You know there are no more dragons." Mam's words were both bitter and sorrowful.

So her parents had told her, but Cami did not feel that was so. She was sure she heard one murmuring and shifting as she drifted off to sleep each night. But Mam always said it was the wind through the trees.

"Then you'll keep me safe with your magic."

Her mother groaned and Popi glanced over his shoulder, looking fiercer than even the embrils. "We have no time for this, Bayel.... Listen to your mother, child, now."

Mam shushed him and took Cami's hands, unfolding them from the pouch. "It is like our secret paintings," she said, her face gone red, her voice strained, "the way we hide special things in the picture so only certain people can find them...do you understand?"

Cami shook her head, her frown deepening. One tear escaped down her cheek.

"We must hide you, daughter. You are one of the special things. Draigbyr is not secret anymore, so now you go to the sanctuary, where Brother Rolfo will keep you safe."

"You come, too," Cami said, the solution so simple to her that she wondered why it was not already so. "We can go together." She smiled, her face bright with hope though tears still hovered in her eyes.

Her father spoke from behind her, his hand trembling as it rested upon her shoulder. "I am sorry, little one. They can sense our magic; they would find us too easily. Now come, we must hurry."

Another tear escaped. Cami sniffed and tried to rub the drop away on her other shoulder. She looked at her mother with pleading eyes, too frightened to look at her father. "You were going to tell me the story of the dragon's jewels today."

Camirel found herself crushed against Mam's chest in a brief, tight hug. "Soon, my emberling, I will tell that tale soon, but for now you must go wait for me. Promise you will wait for me...." Mam's soft words were all but drowned out by the sound of someone running through the undergrowth, crashing and stumbling and occasionally swearing in a voice that sounded like Rolfo.

"'Ware! She comes!" he called out.

Further in the distance someone laughed, but not a happy laugh. It was wrong, cruel, and the sound of it made Cami cringe.

Both parents turned, stricken expressions on their faces. "Mala!"

The name was unfamiliar, but Cami felt her parents' panic, their dread. Her father—for the first time she could remember—cursed, and then pulled them both to their feet. "Now! There is no more time."

Cami heard him muttering, felt him draw magic to his call. Mam sketched runes upon the air until it burned with them. Camirel was startled by the spells they readied. They were dangerous, deadly spells. As likely to do harm to the caster as to the one they would unleash them upon. That her parents would wield such spells now spoke more urgency to her than any of their earlier pleading.

"Bayel! Get her clear," Popi yelled.

Before Mam could do as he ordered, Rolfo came stumbling out of the trees. There was an angry red burn along his wrist and scorch marks all over his robes. He held up a talisman hung around his neck. Imprinted upon it was a flaming dragon. "I swear to you she'll not find us. None of the water witches will."

Without another word he took Cami into his arms. As they fled back through the forest, she felt more of her parents' magic gathering until the air crackled and smelt scorched. Though she could not see for the trees and the distance, Cami strained to look back, praying for a glimpse of her parents hurrying after them.

They did not. As Brother Rolfo settled her on his waiting horse and mounted behind her, the crackle in the air ended in a sharp crack. A roar followed, and the sky lit up with flame. He swore and prodded the horse into a frantic gallop.

Camirel's childhood ended in chaos.

Ten years later

Draigbyr summoned.

The call was not new to Camirel; she had felt it throughout the years, faintly in the background of her life as she grew up and served the brethren at Mabet. It was but a murmur then. It had not been time. She'd been too young, not yet fully come into her magic.

Now, she heard its call deep within the pulse of her blood and answered it. She'd journeyed to the ember oak forest despite the sorrow waiting for her there. She was the last of the Celdraig. Or a daughter of that order, anyway. That legacy bore obligations she must assume.

Camirel stood at the threshold of the forest pondering her next step. These were not tame woods and she no longer had her father by her side, as she always had before.

The trees were called ember oaks because the sap ran hot in them year-round. Some said the massive trees were so large they sent their roots deep into the ground, drawing their heat from the earthfire at the hearts of the surrounding mountains. Others swore that they were not trees at all but the remnants of fallen dragons filled with their fire. Either way, one did not rest a hand casually against those trunks. If one were human, at any rate; it was said to have brought pleasure to the dragons.

When those great beasts still graced the earth, this had been their haven. Or so her parents had told her. The dragons had made their homes in the deep caverns at the heart of the surrounding mountains, but had played here among the trees, frolicking beneath the boughs. It was easy to picture the magical creatures among these giants. Cami liked those stories. She'd heard them countless times. Her parents had shared the teaching of her, the lore interspersed between lessons of runecasting and woodcraft.

The echo of their voices still spoke to her heart. She shuddered, and along with the breeze that wended through the trees, she felt the chill of unrealized tears upon her cheeks, tasted their bitter salt upon her lips. How she missed her parents.

With practiced discipline, Cami turned her mind from those dark thoughts and called on the knowledge she had learned from Popi and Mam, and later Brother Rolfo. She focused on her surroundings and nothing more. With her mind she reached out to shape the forest magic. She felt it wrap around her as she disappeared to normal senses. So shielded, she stepped across the tree line, leaving no footprint and stirring no branch, and still she felt the weight of someone…something watching at her back.

The dragons may have been gone, but other predators—on two legs or four—were known to call this forest their home. With a slow, careful shuffle of her feet, Cami turned, first looking the way she'd come, then closely observing the forest. Prey animals crept unhurried through the underbrush and scurried with more deliberation higher up the tree boles, heading for the canopy far overhead. They showed no more than a normal caution, though, and certainly did not freeze and fade into the background as they would with an active threat nearby.

Most of her journey through the forest was uneventful. She never quite lost the sense of being watched, but neither was she accosted. Out of caution, she kept a defensive spell ready, her fingers tingling with the magic, her ears straining to hear any betraying sound.

Abruptly, she stopped as the change in her surroundings registered. Mostly she took note of the burnt remains of ember oak saplings. Her mind supplied the hard-edged memory of her parents' final spell. Of the way it shattered and tore the very air asunder. The way the sky had burned like a thousand sunsets at its casting. This was where her parents had fallen. And it still bore the mark as if it had happened only moments past.

The blackened trunks, curled by the intense heat that had seared them at her parents' death, gave the tree line the appearance of being edged in black lace, as if the very forest mourned their passing. The branches rattled and clacked as Cami stopped several yards from the original boundary of the clearing, trembling at this reminder of her shattered past. She imagined she could smell burnt cinders on the air. Impossible.

Irrational. And yet, her fingers went to the pouch hidden beneath her smock for comfort.

Driven by her pleading, Rolfo had come back to search for her parents once he had gotten Cami to safety. He found their ashes—how he knew, Cami could not say, but she did not doubt him.

She'd felt their passing.

He'd also found the remains of Mala, the one with whom her parents had done battle, the water witch's nature preserving limb if not life. At least that specter had not loomed over Camirel's days.

Rolfo had brought Cami a small bundle of ashes in memorial.

The carefully wrapped token nestled with the stone in her pouch.

In the long, lonely nights when she'd first been sundered from her parents, she'd talked to the pouch—the stone and the ashes—every day. It was her last link with them. At first she begged forgiveness; certain if she had not resisted leaving their sacrifice would not have come about. But later, as her sorrow eased, she told the stone tales of her days, her problems, or just recounted what she'd learned at her parents' knees, stories of the might and wonder of dragons, of the magic that filled them and the beauty of them on the wing—though this, neither she nor her parents had ever seen. She'd even made up stories of her own, including countless variations on the story of the dragon's jewels her mother had never gotten to tell her. It helped Camirel bear the loss, to imagine them still with her in some way.

Now added to the pouch was Brother Rolfo's dragon talisman, given to her at his death. His passing freed her to answer the call that now brought her here to Draigbyr.

She took a moment to offer a prayer to the First Mother for the souls of her parents and Brother Rolfo, as well as for her own guidance and protection.

Almost in answer, there was a sound behind her, faint and indistinct.

Cami spun around, then froze and drew a sharp breath.

A pack of embrils—lizards the size of two wild boars end to end, only not nearly so pleasant in disposition—spread out among the trees. The sight was an eerie echo of that long-ago day. Then they appeared as an honor guard; now they looked like nothing so much as brush beaters.

If so, Cami would hate to see the huntsman.

They walked with more power than grace, their legs well-muscled and short, their backs thick and their heads crested with a bony plate, giving them a superficial resemblance to paintings of true dragons she had seen. Very superficial. Their skulls were shaped more like a horse's than an antelope's—as a dragon's was—and they had no tails or wings, though a sort of sail-like flap of skin tapered from the knee joint of their front legs to their back hips, which were set lower than their front shoulders. She avoided looking too closely at their well-clawed feet.

Powerful beasts, not pretty, or smart, she told herself, though their gazes were disconcerting.

She wondered if they sensed her, despite her shielding. A tentative effort to slide around the edge of their semicircle drew a growl from the lead embril. Cami halted, conceding that her shielding had been bested. She loosed her hold on her spells and stood very still.

A tremor shook her as childhood memory clashed with the present.

They only liked dragon people. Would they recognize her as Celdraig?

The largest, progressing slightly ahead of the others, stopped within two feet of where she stood. He flared his crest, which must have been made of more than one plate to move so. The creature then gave a toss of its muzzle in the direction she'd been heading and voiced a deep-throated grumble. The others echoed the sound. The message indisputable, Cami turned and resumed walking. Her silent escort moved forward to flank her, the leader walking close enough she could just brush his back with her fingertips if she were of a mind to.

She wasn't so foolish.

Twilight had just kissed the treetops when Cami finally exited the thicket bordering the forest. It had grown dense and deep without her father there to prune it back from the forest edge.

She shivered and told herself it was because of the night's increasing chill, though she was still too close to the trees for that to be so. In the distance she could just make out the silhouette of Draigbyr, the small, secluded keep where she'd been raised. As she stood there, unmoving, the embrils faded away back into the forest, huffing and trilling in farewell.

All but the one beside her.

That one nuzzled her hand. The warmth of its skin was both startling and welcome. The creature flung its head up and back, similar to its guiding gesture earlier.

Cami frowned. She wasn't quite sure, but it seemed to be telling her to mount. Impossible. Edging away, she tried to step into the open on her own. The embril growled, moving with blinding speed to block her path, head raised and weaving in agitation. Its eyes glowed and flared like stirred coals. The intelligence in them unnerved her. Again, it drew close and nuzzled her hand, followed by the head gesture.

This time Cami complied, laying herself across the broad, rough back, clinging like an opossum kit, with both arms and legs. It was like hugging a massive barrel. One wrapped in sanded paper. Her position brought her face close to the creature's startling warmth. She had not realized how bitter the night air was beyond the influence of the ember oaks until her back shivered violently while, in contrast, her front basked.

Closing her eyes and laying her head down, Cami had to wonder if this were all a dream. It was so surreal. And yet she felt at peace. Safe in a way she had not felt since her parents had informed her they were sending her away. The journey—across miles and years—had been so long. She was weary. Soon the rhythm of the embril's walking and the warmth of its body sent Camirel drifting into a half slumber. She woke some time later with a gasp as the creature stopped, the specter of that long-ago flight invading her rest.

The embril grumbled when she clutched at it with frantic fingers. It shifted and stood with an air of waiting, but not patience. Cami relaxed her grip and squeezed her eyes closed.

She did not need sight to know where the beast had brought her. Her peculiar mount had delivered her to the keep. Beneath her, the embril coughed, an annoyed sound, and she hastily slid from its back.

"Thank you," she murmured. The creature trilled in response as it disappeared into the night. Cami did not turn to the gaping arch leading into Draigbyr until the embril was gone. When she did, her hand came up to brush a brighter patch of stone in the outer wall. She remembered helping her father gather stones for the repair. That one memory brought a flood of others until Cami nearly went to her knees. Most were times of joy and peace, happy memories but for those of that final day. Not for the first time she wondered, if she had not resisted so, would her parents be here with her this day?

Before the weight of her long-felt guilt could take hold she heard a rumble, like a rock pile shifting. It came from the keep. Slowly turning, she stared at the main entrance to the enclave. The opening was massive, five times the height of a tall man and four times his measure wide, were he lying down.

The doors were open.

A warm current from within, carried the scent of old cinders. It wrapped around her and, though her nerves remained taut, she was not afraid. Another rumble sounded, somehow soothing and definitely impatient. She wanted to believe it was the timbers of the keep shifting, but as when she was younger, she could sense the being responsible for the sound. A ripple of fear-entwined wonder went through her.

At Cami's neck, the pouch hidden beneath her smock heated like a glowing coal, over-warm, but not quite uncomfortable against her skin. And still she did not walk through the arch. In the darkness within Draigbyr's walls, she began to make out two patches of sullen glow, like banked embers among a hearth's ash. Then the embers kindled and flared. Shimmered like flame reflected on clear glass.

Every muscle in Camirel tensed and she could not help but gasp. Her mind stammered a silent denial of the coiled shape not quite revealed by the glow. She was unsure she felt awe, or fear. The two were quite similar.

I would see you closer, demanded a gravelly voice in her head. Beneath the impression of disuse, there was the crackle and snap Cami normally associated with the hearth fire.

Stunned, she did not move.

Now!

The warmth withdrew and then washed over her once more, like a breath drawn and exhaled.

Cami took a trembling step forward. What she'd willfully assumed was a fallen timber lifted from the ground, revealing a taloned digit that could be mistaken for nothing else. Her chest seized a moment, the fear uncontrollable, despite the reverent tales she'd been reared upon. The talon came to rest below the hollow of her throat, just where the pouch lay hidden. At its touch, the gemstone blazed uncomfortably hot, even through the leather encasing it.

You have returned to us, lost one.

Cami shifted among the rubble in an effort to look about without taking her eyes from the dragon. She could not believe that those words were for her, but then, to whom did the great one speak? A narrow, graceful head, frilled in a manner that called the embrils to mind, darted forward into the moonlight. Cami would have screamed had she the voice for it. The head gave the impression of being delicate, despite its size. The teeth did not. Amusement radiated from those alien features. The dragon pinned Cami with a look.

We speak to you both, emberling. The talon brushed Cami's chest, and then again the pouch containing the stone. *Man-child and dragon-child.*

The later words were all but lost upon Cami.

Emberling. Mam had called her emberling. She sobbed and the dragon drew near, head tilted to the side as it considered Cami closer.

A breath of hot wind rushed over her. It took effort not to cringe. Her cheeks heated with shame, for this was not the dragon of her daydreams. Her child's mind had painted a gentler, more benevolent picture. What lay coiled before her was at once more wild and dangerous than anything she could yet imagine, let alone when she'd been a child.

The dragon made a sound deep in its massive throat, as if it sensed her thoughts. It backed away from her, an odd expression of distaste paired with its draconic mien; offense broadcast from each taut muscle.

There is an oath bond between our kind and yours; do you think we would not honor it?

Cami felt six years old again, and chastised for wrongdoing. "W-we thought there were no more dragons. Wh-where have you been?"

Another deep rumble. *Sleeping beneath the mountain.*

Such a simple, matter-of-fact answer! It startled a laugh from Cami. She clapped her hand over her mouth and tensed. Had she given further offense? As she waited, her gaze ran over what she could see of the dragon. So massive. So magnificent. The paintings were a travesty in comparison. Oh, how she wished Popi and Mam could have been here. Again a sob caught in her throat, the wonder of the moment conflicting with her instinctive fear and long-felt sorrow.

The dragon lowered itself to the ground. Its head shook slowly from side to side, for all the world so like Mam at her most exasperated that another laugh escaped Cami's throat, a touch of the hysterical about it. *Sit,* the dragon ordered. The impatience was clear.

Camirel complied.

I would hear your tale, emberling.

Before Cami could speak her story the dragon reached out a talon. Cami tensed, her breath caught in her breast. The instant the talon tip touched her head, Cami's life unfolded like a melt-flooded river. The joy and the pain of growing up and the lonely years since, the memories and horrors, the hopes and dreams...things Cami had long since forgot, things she'd never realized she'd known. It was all there and minutely examined. Camirel shivered and shook with the shock of it. Her eyes closed and she could not contain a bittersweet keen.

The talon hastily pulled away.

For a moment there was silence. They sat there merely breathing and, to Cami, the night seemed to grow darker and more frigid.

Then the dragon's voice spoke softly in her head.

Come, young one. She—for she, she was—swept back her folded wings, baring forelimbs not too dissimilar to Cami's, were the talons disregarded. They opened slowly, gently. *You are yet a child and weary. Rest against my warmth, and I will tell you a tale.*

Cami would have protested being called a child, only there was no mistaking the contrition in the offer. The dragon's heart was as open as her arms and Cami could see no deceit there, no harm wished. Beyond weary, she stepped forward, climbed the dragon's coils and lay herself down. The arms and both sets of wings closed about her to form a toasty bower for her rest. It had the feel of coming home. Sighing, Cami murmured, "Which one?" in response to the dragon's offer.

Silence again reigned, though not uncomfortably. Cami held her breath and waited.

The one you were promised. Only the truth of it.

And so Cami settled in, fresh tears washing away old sorrow as she learned of the link between dragons and gems.... No. Not gems, emberlings, dragon young cradled deep within the belly of the earth—the First Mother. The two were not the same, though they appeared so.

Long ago, before the time of men, the dragon murmured in soft, soothing tones. *The First Mother had the Fire-Borne as Her child. She cradled it deep in Her belly, warmed it with the earthfire deep in the heart of Her. As it formed and grew, She gave it the name of Dragon and whispered to the emberling lullabies of what it was to become. It learned the joy of flying first at Her words, long before it even had wings; it heard the glory of roaring as She spoke it, before the emberling's lungs had even formed.*

Cami was held rapt by both story and teller. Images formed in her mind as the dragon spoke. Weariness dissolved as wonder grew. Without even thinking, Cami's arms came up to wrap around the limb she rested against, as she would have done with Mam. The dragon's chest rumbled beneath her and Cami sensed the pleasure in the sigh. She continued her tale while Cami laid her head down upon its butter-soft hide.

*The emberling was a long time in learning, the Dragon form being as complex as it is beautiful. The First Mother nurtured

Her child until it was ready for the world, then slowly pushed it up from its cradle.

It rose to the surface until Dragon erupted from its womb upon plumes of earthfire, flying into the sky fully formed and magnificent, but never forgetting its First Mother.

*And thus from the beginning of time until the end of it, the Dragon vowed to bring its emberlings down into the earthfire and present them to the First Mother for Her to cradle them while both Mother and Dragon murmured lullabies to the emberlings of what they would one day be.

*For age upon age that was the way of it. But as happens when time passes a younger race appeared. This one, borne of all elements in equal measure, walked upon two legs and had not the blessing of wings.

Dragon and its kind lived in harmony with the new ones for a time. However, as the race of Man grew and spread, they learned a liking for things found cradled in the earth: gold and gems and other metals. Being a short-lived race, some were not content for the First Mother to reveal her treasures in her time; they tore them from her depths and claimed them for their own, unmindful of the harm they did. In their taking, they uncradled the emberlings nestled in the earth, confusing them for common gemstones.

Cami gasped and clutched the forelimb closer, her heart aching at the tale. The dragon rested its muzzle lightly against her head, again as Mam had once done, before continuing:

*And thus grew the rift between Dragon and Man. But Man was many and Dragons few, and without the emberlings their number would not grow. Some among the race of Man did not hold with the practice of raping the earth and harming Dragons. Those few took a blood-vow to the older race. They learned the Dragons' tales that none be lost, they did for the Dragons what service they were best suited to, but mostly they traveled the world of Man seeking out the stolen young. These were called the Celdraig.

*They were but few and, when discovered, persecuted by their own kind, who would not give up their stolen treasures. The thieves hunted and slaughtered Celdraig and Dragon both until but one Dragon remained, sorely injured and alone. That one hid itself beneath the mountain to heal.

*The order of the Celdraig retreated to the wilderness keeps they had established. There they waited many generations for Dragon to return, letting no lore be forgotten as their seekers searched for emberlings trapped in the world of Man.

While beneath its mountain, the Dragon slept and healed and dreamt of its' lost emberlings and the special child of the Celdraig who would bring them home.

The last words were flavored with both sorrow and joy.

Cami started to speak, and then thought better of it, only to open her mouth again, moments later. Again trepidation overwhelmed her and the words remained unspoken.

You have the scent of the Celdraig, child, but not the feel of one oath-bound, the dragon spoke into her silence. *We are weary, our time upon this earth soon done. We have waited long for you. Would you enter an oath with us?*

Instinctively, Camirel quaked inside. She thought she knew what was being asked. Feared so, anyway, and though taking up the mantle of the Celdraig had been her greatest wish, she was sadly unprepared for it, her learning incomplete, her understanding clearly flawed. She wanted with all her heart to uphold the honor of the Celdraig. She feared with all her heart she could not do it justice.

No, child...no, emberling, as your own first mother has named you, you are meant for your own glory, if you would have it.

Camirel quivered from her skin to her core. Her breath quickened and she could scarcely credit what she thought was being asked of her.

Our emberling, the dragon murmured as her head lowered over Cami's shoulder to nuzzle the pouch, *will need to be more than a teller of tales when we are gone.*

The daughter of the Celdraig gasped. Her heart raced in pace with her mind, both frenetic at the concept she could scarcely conceive, though the dragon fed images into Cami's thoughts along with the words.

Reason could not grasp this, but her spirit could. Her soul knew this was her destined course, spoken into her dreams long before her life had been sundered. She found she was not afraid to share the emberling's transformation. Camirel stood and the dragon rose with her.

She was startled to note that the sun already lit the sky. Lifting her face to the golden glow, Cami drew the morning air into her lungs, wondered what life would hold for her once she was Fire-Borne.

The dragon came to stand behind her in the dawn. A wingtip lifted to block out the sky. The underwing's folds closed around and tight, drawing Cami against hard, muscled flesh the texture of sun-scorched sand. The air shattered with a booming sound as if the earth itself cracked asunder. The massive forewings had deployed. For Cami, the underwings' folds muffled the sound until her head only pounded. It matched her heart's beat when dragon muscle bunched and flexed, propelling them into the air.

They were aloft; Cami could not breathe with the fear-tinged wonder of it all. Her chest was tight, as was her skin, as if sun-burned. It was the dragon's heat. A mere nothing compared to the earthfire soon to cradle her.

"What should I call you?" Cami half wondered to herself, not expecting the dragon to hear the wind-stolen words. She was wrong in this as well.

Last Mother, the proud dragon's voice murmured in her thoughts as she carried Cami and the emberling deep within the cradle of the earthfire, leaving them safe in the arms of the First Mother, before settling in to murmur their lullabies.

TRANSCENDENCE

"I open the door of heaven."

—The Goddess Sesheta,
The Book of Coming Forth By Day

HAVE YOU EVER GAZED INTO THE HEART OF A STAR?

I have. You are blind to anything else forever after, no matter if your eyes are yet capable of seeing. The memory dazzles your vision, your mind, leaves you in open-mouthed awe at the wonder of it. No commonplace sight that the universe may offer can hope to compare.

I did not intend to alter my perception so radically. I had no choice in this.

My name is Sesheta.

It was not always, but any other name I may have laid claim to is long lost to me. Some may know, might even tell you if you ask, but otherwise it would not occur to them, blinded as they are, by the lingering light of that star.

In darkness...I shine.

This likewise was not always so.

On the day of my rebirth, I was led to a chamber in the ship no other was allowed to access. Etched into the hatch was a single word: Library. I wondered at that as the simple portal opened. Inside was dark, near complete, but for a pinpoint of light on the far wall. The atmosphere was stale, heavy with the scent of dust, despite the steady rumble of cycled air.

"Go," my keeper ordered. A gentle shove to my back sent me forward fearing to stumble, fearing what might obstruct my path, unknown, unyielding...but there was nothing.

"Go, child. You must. There is no other...."

He was ancient and all to him were 'child,' no matter that I was no untried youth.

I went forward, though I could not bring myself to anything but timid steps. My breath trembled in my chest. I remember this. I can yet feel the slick skin of sweat coating me, clinging my clothes to my body, chilling any bare skin. Nothing came up hard against my shins...nothing sent me tumbling to the deck. The point of light grew closer, if no bigger.

Don't ask me how I knew. Such details simply are since I took up my mantle.

"You must look through," the keeper murmured at my back, distant in both space and my awareness. "Place your eye to the hole."

His voice sounded sad to me, but beneath that, hope and dread and uncertainty colored his words. It was an echo of my own heart.

Fearful, but obedient, I advanced until my breasts flattened against riveted steel. The placement of the glass-covered hole forced my head to bow in compliance.

It was the last time I would assume such a position.

I saw everything and nothing. Every color of light flooded my vision and all the knowledge of the universe was at my command, wrote itself into my very being until such a simple thing as a name scarce had room for itself, it was buried so deep. For an instant and forever I heard the music to which all light dances, the singing of stars and the beating of their hearts, felt my sweat-dampened hair ruffled by the solar winds, tasted the bitter cold of space, scented by the aeons.

I saw forever in the heart of that star.

Do you wonder that I was so changed?

Tst! Pay attention!

I rose that day from where I'd crumpled with my clothes, myself, my fears burned away. I turned back to face my keeper. By the glow of my bare skin I became aware of the pictures on the chamber walls, etched glyphs, symbols of another age at once both strange and known to me. They were obsolete, lost in the shadow of all knowledge crowding my thoughts.

I retraced my earlier footsteps, no longer timid, no longer blind, though I still could not say if the sight was that of my eyes. I stopped at the threshold where my former keeper had abased himself. I brushed my fingertips across the crown of his bowed head. The fine strands of his aged hair shimmered a moment and the ancient gasped, his body taut and trembling.

Such is common for those star-touched.

Hair thickened, gleamed with an ebon hue recalled from long-ago years, skin smoothed, and twisted joints straightened until ageless youth rest beneath my hand.

"Rise," I told him who had for so long remained faithful, "and attend me."

We walked across the heavens, opened the doors of transcendence, ushered a great many souls.

I can tell by your eyes you would ask me why, if only you dared. I will tell you. Mankind was easily lost among the heavens, without someone to guide the way.

Ages passed unnoticed. Time means little when starsong echoes in your ear.

He is gone now, in case you wonder. They are all gone, but for my remembering.

I am tired, child...and there is no other...place your eye to the hole.

FROM THE AUTHOR

Thank you for reading *Transcendence.* I hope you enjoyed the book. If you did, the greatest thanks you can give would be posting a review some place where other potential readers can learn about the book.

I love to hear from readers, so please do feel free to email me as well at greenfirephoenix@aol.com.

Best,

Danielle Ackley-McPhail

ON THE WINGS
OF AN ANGEL

CAN'T SAY AS I DIDN'T RECKON I WAS GOING MAD. IT WOULDN'TA surprised me if'n it were so. I already reckoned I was in hell, that's enough to turn anyone's mind....

But first, I call myself Miss Sadie Angelina Carlisle, though I don't bother much with any name but the middle one anymore. Not since takin' up residence at the Lucky Strike Saloon in Dead Dog, Montana, anyway. See, the proprietor, Mr. Clayton, he says men are happier pretendin' they're keepin' company with an angel, rather than a common whore. I do as I'm told, else Mr. Clayton might forget he likes havin' an angel below stairs temptin' and teasin' the custom, rather than just another girl entertainin' above stairs. Men don't pay near so much for common. They have to save up for an angel, even a fallen one; unless they hit a strike. That ain't happened yet. Till then, I sing.

"Sadie! Sun's settin', quit wool-gatherin' and get yourself into your rig afore I find someone else as fits it!"

Lordie, but that black-hearted Clayton can bellow. I can't help but shudder at his bald-faced threat though. That happen, and I might as well drop the name Angel too. Ain't none of us outta reach of his temper. I'd do to remember that. And I reckon he's been givin' me looks makin' me wonder will I be below stairs much longer anyhow. Looks that make me think he's tired of waitin' for a prospector with that big strike to come along. I've no doubt I've only been spared entertainin' the custom 'cause there ain't anyone come in able to pay the price Mr. Clayton has set on my innocence.

I flinch at the thought and rush to do as I'm bid, my mind near jibberin' half-formed pleas for deliverance, but not hardly expectin' it will ever come. I'm already wearin' my white satin gown and matchin' slippers with the thick leather soles; now for the rest. Quick-like I beckon over Shelby, one of the above stairs ladies, for some help 'cause I plum can't suit up all myself.

See, our Mr. Clayton, he's into mods and mechanicals. Show him somethin' with gears and I reckon he starts breathin' like he's been with a five-dollar whore. There are bits of invention all over the saloon I can scarce make sense of. They're most nothin' much but tinker's toys like the little metal birds what can't fly, but sing pertier than me...if'n only ever just one song, and miniature carriages made for Cook's son movin' by themselves on tiny puffs of steam....The bartender is flesh enough, but there ain't a bottle of liquor to be seen—nor broke, if'n the custom gets rowdy. Drinks is portioned out by a clockwork contraption of gears and pipes that can take a dent and keep on pourin' the next drink in just as precise a measure as the last. Then there's the player piano what plays itself like any other, but ain't no crank involved, just lotsa steam and valves and whatnot. It's an amazin' thing of copper and brass instead of wood, with gold-plated keys, and not soundin' no more tinny than any other upright I ever heard.

But all of that ain't nothin' compared to my rig.

I can't help but think about that with longin' and loathin' mixed, rememberin' when and how it came to be. There were a tinker what come through town. An odd, dirt-smudged, little man what made me more nervous than an uncooped hen after dark. The first he scurried into the saloon and looked his fill at every one of us, we felt near stripped bare down to our very souls, though there weren't nothin' to it that was lecherous or mean. More like Mr. Edward S. Curtis, what came through with his pho-tography equipment once on his way to visit the Blackfoot Injuns; he used to look just so at near everythin', like he was searchin' for the perfect picture it would make.

I swear if I didn't feel the tinker's gaze linger just the same on me, though I can't fathom why. I was a young'n yet, and nothin' special to catch the custom's eye. Like now, I sang for my place, when I weren't cleanin'.

Was the tinker first called me Angel, with a nervous-makin' gleam in his eye—like he saw more to me than I rightly knew was there—and him not even knowin' my given name. That amused Mr. Clayton so much it stuck.

Then that there tinker set to catch Mr. Clayton's attention with such contraptions as you can't never imagine and I can scarce describe. The things that came out of his sack...my Lord, it was a sight. The two of 'em spent more'n a piece of time with their heads together, hagglin'. Hard to say who hoodwinked who, but both men walked away with a smarmy smile.

The tinker stayed a spell after. He puttered around in the cellar until near all you heard afore hours was bangin' and the hiss of steam, but evenin's he ended up in the saloon pesterin' me. Askin' questions and starin' me up and down mutterin' "not yet" under his breath, like maybe I didn't quite match the picture in his head.

The questions made me more nervous than the mutterin'. They was dangerous questions: What did I wish for? What would I rather be? I was too feared then to speak, but my heart...it was cryin' out to be free! There was nothin' I wanted more than deliverance. The tinker just nodded and gave me a wink, like he heard what I ain't said, before disappearin' again back down ta the cellar.

I wanted to believe. Darn near convinced myself he could do anythin'—includin' save me—after seein' him tinker with one of the songbirds what always sang particularly sad. I'd felt my forehead for a fever when he closed up its tiny back and brushed a finger over it what set it glitterin' and glowin' like pixie dust. Then...that little bird took wing, flyin' out the window never again to be seen! It trilled a happy song as it escaped.

A *different* song.

That's when I had to wonder was I goin' mad.

And still, I took to hopin' then, though ain't nothin' ever come of it.

Afore he left for good, that little man cornered me in the pantry whiles I was helpin' Cook with supper. He stood there, hunched and taut, again starin' me up and down all familiar-like. "Don't you worry...for now, you're safer here," he'd murmured, his head side-cocked and his eyes narrowed like he was lookin' again for his own perfect picture. "But remember, when that's no longer so...Angels were made to fly."

His words left me ashiver in a way I declare I'd never felt afore or since.

To this day, I can hear him whisperin' that, and would swear on my dead ma's Bible if'n I had it, that I sometimes still spy him in the shadows, watchin', eyes narrowed just so, though I know he's gone. Quite mad, true, I but can't help but wishin' that mayhap the tinker were right and I'll have me a chance to fly away.

Anyhow, by the time the tinker finally moved along after considerable time spent in the cellar, the parlor had acquired somethin' wondrous new.

Even now I can't help but hold my breath whiles Shelby unlocks my special cabinet. The thing is tall, clear up to the above stairs ceilin'. The whole front and sides foldin' back with fancy paintin' everywhere on the inside, like you would imagine heaven to be, all but for what Mr. Clayton calls the new-matic tube; a brass pipe runnin' down the center, shiny as the day the tinker set it in place.

My rig just hangs there in the middle of the air like someone forgot to paint in the angel, 'ceptin' for its halo and wings—I ain't ever yet been tall enough for that halo to perch proper atop my head. Each time I see The Angel it dazzles me, so's I always near forget how much I dread to buckle the contraption on.

Ain't got no choice, though. Never did. Mr. Clayton says an Angel's gotta have wings if'n anyone's gonna believe she fell from heaven.

An' mayhap they do, when I'm singin'—if I can be forgiven the smallest bit of pride. Savin' for my voice, there's precious little about me that ain't common, or so my pa use to say. 'Course given this rig here—and the presence of the above stairs ladies— I'd be a mite surprised did the gents notice a thing about myself, no matter that I'm hoverin' in thin air above their heads lookin' near the picture of angelic. (Times like that, I can't help but remember the tinker's words...and that little metal songbird. My heart goes all tight each time I do....)

Oh glory, just to look at it.... Wings made of gen-u-ine swan feathers brushed light like with gold. Mr. Clayton's after callin' it guilt, then laughin' his fool ass off like'n he said somethin' funny. Which, given the nature of his establishment....

I'm mighty fond of those perty wings. The corset, though...that there's a pure torment to wear. I must stand just so the entire time if'n I'm to have enough air to breathe, let alone sing as I'm expected. I do imagine were not the whole thing latched on to the new-matic tube I could plum fly away. I reckon I wish that were so somethin' fierce.

Right now, the only thing protectin' my virtue is my singin', and my not-quite-generous curves. I'm afeared that won't be so for long bein' I've had to dodge more'n a few grabbin' hands of late.

Before Mr. Clayton can bellow once more, I step up onto the platform makin' up the bottom of the cabinet, and though I mostly feel forsaken, I lift up a prayer to the God my ma once swore by. After all, in a manner, she'd been delivered, even if her passin' had left me to bear pa alone, if'n only for a short spell, before he foisted me off on Mr. Clayton.

I step into the frame, careful of the many danglin' straps and buckles, makin' sure my feet set just so on the narrow brass plate they're meant to perch on. I shudder to recall the time they'd slipped from that square. The breath was near squeezed out of me. I've learned to be particular since. My eyes close all on their own and I draw deep and full till my lungs near want to burst as Shelby cages me in that rig of iron ribbin', white leather, and polished brass. Otherwise there ain't no room to breathe once the contraption's buckled tight.

Those lookin' on see nothin' but perty; from the moment I'm buckled in till they free me, I'm nigh in pain, forced to stand straight and still as Sundy service else scald my back on the gleamin' brass pole behind me.

It was a wonder I could ever sing a note, but derned if I don't put the nightingale to shame each and every night when I put on The Angel and dangle there in 'heaven' to give the custom a show, and that ain't no boast.

I hear the clunk of the lever bein' pulled across the room, followed by the hiss of steam warmin' the ledge beneath my feet. There's the whir of shiftin' gears as the wings spread, and I feel just a bit giddy as I rise up in the air above the platform. Can't help but wonder maybe this time I won't stop in the middle. Mayhap I'll be crushed against the ceilin' or, mayhap I'll sure enough fly away. There ain't no holdin' back my giggle at that. But then the sound of the hiss changes and my perch slows, then stops.

I feel it then. A shiver down m'spine. Familiar-like, enough that I expect I'd see him...the tinker...if'n my eyes weren't shut. I imagine I hear that little songbird as well, and I let my eyes drift open to see did either of 'em really come back.

But all that's there is the familiar sight of The Angel framed in the mirror behind the bar. Only not quite the same as always....

Just a tiny gasp escapes me and I forget to look for what I expected.

For the first time ever, that there halo's just behind my head and The Angel's starin' back, all brown-gold curls and creamy white skin, with a tiny waist and a bosom to put the above stairs ladies to shame. She's wearin' my face.

But it ain't that what startles me. It were Mr. Clayton holdin' up a walnut-size nugget of gold with a shit-eatin' grin on his face. Standin' next to him was a grubby, overlarge miner smellin' rank even from here.

No longer able to deny my days of bein' safe were done, I recoil, only to have fierce heat sear my back.

I don't smell scorched satin or burnt flesh, as I'd expect. I smell a garden like my ma use to have, and again I hear that tiny metal bird. The burnin's gone afore I even draw breath to cry out and in the mirror I swear that pipin' hot brass ain't at my back no more.

A gasp rises from every throat in the room and if I weren't so scared I'd laugh as their eyes go wide, but I'm afraid to move, afraid to fall. Then somethin' brushes my shoulders, sends them tinglin' like they been long asleep and only just wakin' up. I start to glitter. I shiver again and a flush steals over me. Wisps of steam curl at my feet like soft white clouds, no longer overwarm.

Then...quiet by my ear, barely louder'n a breath...I hear the tinker's sigh-like whisper, "Now...be free."

I feel like I imagine that bird did, afraid to believe...afraid not to.

My body shakes at the tinker's words, in eager-like tremors from head to toe. Mayhap I imagine it...mayhap I truly am mad...but somethin' sparks off my skin, rises up from my bones and sets me aglow. I remember the songbird as I feel the sudden flex of wings at my back, the bunchin' of muscles I ain't ever used. I open my mouth and out pours a terrible, wonderful, glorious sound.

As The Angel sings, the buckles fall away, and m'iron cage rains to the sawdust-covered floor in pieces as gilded feathers lift me to the sky.

ABOUT THE AUTHOR

Award-winning author and editor Danielle Ackley-McPhail has worked both sides of the publishing industry for longer than she cares to admit. In 2014 she joined forces with husband Mike McPhail and friend Greg Schauer to form her own publishing house, eSpec Books (www.especbooks.com).

Her published works include seven novels, *Yesterday's Dreams, Tomorrow's Memories, Today's Promise, The Halfling's Court, The Redcaps' Queen, Daire's Devils*, and *Baba Ali and the Clockwork Djinn*, written with Day Al-Mohamed. She is also the author of the solo collections *A Legacy of Stars, Consigned to the Sea, Flash in the Can,* and *Transcendence*, the non-fiction writers' guide, *The Literary Handyman*, and is the senior editor of the *Bad-Ass Faeries* anthology series, *Gaslight & Grimm, After Punk,* and *Footprints in the Stars*. Her short stories are included in numerous other anthologies and collections.

She is a member of Broad Universe, a writer's organization focusing on promoting the works of women authors in the speculative genres.

In addition to her literary acclaim, she crafts and sells original costume horns under the moniker The Hornie Lady, and homemade candied ginger in a variety of flavors under the brand Ginger KICK! at literary conventions, on commission, and wholesale.

Danielle lives in New Jersey with husband and fellow writer, Mike McPhail and three extremely spoiled cats. She can be found on Facebook (Danielle Ackley-McPhail) and Twitter (DMcPhail, BadAssFaeries, eSpecBooks, and TheHornieLady).

To learn more about her work, visit www.sidhenadaire.com or www.especbooks.com.

ALSO FEATURED

Jennifer Brozek is an award-winning editor, game designer, and author. She has worked in the publishing industry since 2004. With the number of edited anthologies, fiction sales, RPG books, and nonfiction books under her belt, Jennifer is often considered a Renaissance woman, but she prefers to be known as a wordslinger and optimist. Read more about her at or follow her on Twitter: @JenniferBrozek.

John G. Hartness is a teller of tales, a righter of wrongs, defender of ladies' virtues, and some people call him Maurice, for he speaks of the pompatus of love. He is the author of The Black Knight Chronicles (Bell Bridge), and creator of the comic horror Bubba the Monster Hunter series and the Big Bad series (Dark Oak Press). John enjoys long walks on the beach, rescuing kittens from trees and recording episodes of his podcast Literate Liquors, where he pairs book reviews and alcoholic drinks in new and ludicrous ways. An avid Magic: the Gathering player, John is strong in his nerd-fu.

John Grant is author of some seventy books, of which about twenty-five are fiction. His "book-length fiction" *Dragonhenge*, illustrated by Bob Eggleton, was shortlisted for a Hugo Award in 2003; its successor was *The Stardragons*. His first story collection, *Take No Prisoners*, appeared in 2004. His anthology *New Writings in the Fantastic* was shortlisted for a British Fantasy Award. In nonfiction, he has coedited with John Clute *The Encyclopedia of Fantasy* and written in their entirety all three editions of *The Encyclopedia of Walt Disney's Animated Characters*.

Among his latest nonfictions have been *Discarded Science, Corrupted Science, Bogus Science* and *Denying Science.* As John Grant he has received two Hugo Awards, the World Fantasy Award, the Locus Award, and various other international literary awards. Under his real name, Paul Barnett, he for a number of years ran the world-famous fantasy-artbook imprint Paper Tiger, for this work earning a Chesley Award and a nomination for the World Fantasy Award. His website is at www.johngrantpaulbarnett.com.

L. Jagi Lamplighter is the author of two young adult fantasies: The Unexpected Enlightenment of Rachel Griffin and The Raven, the Elf, and Rachel. She is also the author of the Prospero's Daughter series: Prospero Lost, Prospero In Hell, and Prospero Regained. She has published numerous articles on Japanese animation and appears in several short story anthologies, including Best of Dreams of Decadence, No Longer Dreams, Coliseum Morpheuon, the Bad-Ass Faeries anthologies (where she is also an assistant editor) and the Science Fiction Book Club's Don't Open This Book.

Misty Massey is the author of Mad Kestrel (Tor), a rollicking fantasy adventure of magic on the high seas, and Kestrel's Voyages, a book of short stories featuring Kestrel and her crew. She is one of the editors of the upcoming anthology The Weird Wild West (eSpec Books) and a featured blogger on Magical Words. You can see more of what Misty's up to at her website, or find her on Facebook and Twitter.

Lillian Cohen-Moore is an award winning editor, and devotes her writing to fiction, journalism and game design. Influenced by the work of Jewish authors and horror movies, she draws on bubbe meises (grandmother's tales) and horror classics for inspiration. She loves exploring and photographing abandoned towns; Lillian spends every fall searching for corn mazes and haunted houses—the spookier the better. She is a member of the Society of Professional Journalists and the Online News Association.

CJ Henderson was the creator of both the Piers Knight supernatural investigator series and the Teddy London occult detective series among many others. He has written over 70 books and/or novels, hundreds and hundreds of short stories and comics and thousands of non-fiction pieces. He is a master of hardboiled suspense as well as raucous comedy, and is not shy about saying so even when sober. For more on this truly fascinating teller of tales, he encourages all to stop in at www.cjhenderson.com. He promises free short stories and more humility. C.J. passed away from lymphoma in July 2014.

Tonia Brown is a Southern author with a penchant for Victorian dead things. Her work ranges from steampunk to romance to humor to horror, and a healthy mix of these genres. She is the author of Badass Zombie Roadtrip and Lucky Stiff from Books of the Dead Press, Sundowners and Skin Trade from Permuted Press, Hauling Ash from Post Hill Press, and the Clockworks and Corsets series from Kinsington Press, as well as the weird western web serial, Railroad! She lives in the backwoods of North Carolina with her genius husband and an ever fluctuating number of cats.

Gail Z. Martin is the prolific author of the epic fantasy Reign of Ash (Orbit Books 2014), urban fantasy Deadly Curiosities, (Solaris Books), set in Charleston, SC and Iron and Blood, a steampunk novel (2015, Solaris Books) co-authored with her husband, Larry N. Martin.

Find her at www.ChroniclesOfTheNecromancer.com, on Twitter @GailZMartin, on Facebook.com/WinterKingdoms, at DisquietingVisions.com blog and GhostInTheMachinePodcast.com. She leads monthly conversations on Goodreads and posts free excerpts of her work on Wattpad.

Paul Levinson, PhD, is Professor of Communication &Media Studies at Fordham University in New York City. His eight non-fiction books, including The Soft Edge (1997), Digital McLuhan (1999), Realspace (2003), Cellphone (2004), and New New Media (2009; 2nd edition, 2012) have been the subject of major articles in The New York Times, Wired, the Christian Science Monitor, and have been translated into ten languages. His science fiction novels include The Silk Code (1999, winner of the Locus Award for Best First Novel), Borrowed Tides (2001), The Consciousness Plague (2002), The Pixel Eye (2003), and The Plot to Save Socrates (2006). His short stories have been nominated for Nebula, Hugo, Edgar, and Sturgeon Awards. Paul Levinson appears on "The O'Reilly Factor" (Fox News), "The CBS Evening News," "NewsHour with Jim Lehrer" (PBS), "Nightline" (ABC), Dylan Ratigan (MSNBC) and numerous national and international TV and radio programs. His 1972 LP, Twice Upon a Rhyme, was re-issued on mini-CD by Big Pink Records in 2009, and was re-issued in a vinyl remastered re-pressing by Sound of Salvation/Whiplash Records in December 2010. He reviews the best of television in his InfiniteRegress.tv blog, writes political and media commentary for Mediaite, and was listed in The Chronicle of Higher Education's "Top 10 Academic Twitterers" in 2009.